THE KNOWLEDGE

THE
KNOWLEDGE

MARK JACKSON

Matador
9 Priory Business Park,
Wistow Road, Kibworth Beauchamp,
Leicestershire. LE8 0RX
Tel: 0116 279 2299
Email: books@troubador.co.uk
Web: www.troubador.co.uk/matador
Twitter: @matadorbooks

ISBN 978 183859 307 0

British Library Cataloguing in Publication Data.
A catalogue record for this book is available from the British Library.

Printed on FSC accredited paper
Printed and bound in Great Britain by 4edge Limited
Typeset in 11pt Minion Pro by Troubador Publishing Ltd, Leicester, UK

Matador is an imprint of Troubador Publishing Ltd

For Nigel and Katie

PROLOGUE

London, 1688

T HE THAMES SPLIT LONDON LIKE A BLACK scar.

It formed a seeping wound between north and south; wealth and neglect. The boatman hunched his shoulders and pulled. Rutter's only concern about the rich, whose palaces and town houses lined the north bank, was the coin he could squeeze from them.

The wooden blades disappeared into the filth of the river. In the moonlight it was a sheet of shifting tar. The Thames stank. To the unaccustomed, it could make your eyes weep, but Rutter was used to it.

He'd grown up on the boats, working them since he was a small boy. His hands and forearms were rigid with slabs of muscle. Although a short man, Rutter seemed bigger as he pulled the boat, his shoulders out of proportion after years of hauling heavier cargo. His left hand was missing two fingers; digits lost in a knife fight when he had been younger and let his temper get the better of him.

The boat carried three men. His passengers were sitting away from him, both muffled garb and voices. But sound carried over water. Periodically, a glint of fine silk at their throats caught the light from the torches that lined the banks of the river. Even in dark cloaks, the two men were marked as rich and powerful.

Torches lined each side of the Thames. On the north bank, were drawn the sharp outlines of the Palace of Westminster and the merchants' palaces. Rutter had his back to the south bank: a wall of warehouses, which stretched for miles down to the naval yards at Greenwich.

They were almost halfway across now. Rutter checked their position and adjusted his angled stroke. Rutter had no hair. His pate was made luminous by the moon each time the clouds passed over it. His charges' hair was long, curled, fashionable. He resisted the urge to spit over the side. Some passengers didn't like that sort of behaviour; it might cost him a tip.

His passengers were arguing.

Rutter could sense the desperation, straining to hear the words as he hauled on the oar:

"Please, Your Majesty. Reconsider, Sire."

There was no point whispering, the river heard everything, thought Rutter grimly. Then it came to him: who he was ferrying tonight. Christ! This time he spat as he felt bile rising.

The King was sitting as though unmoved, his long

gloved fingers clutching a small object in his hands. The Great Seal. A symbol of power, but more than that, it was the King's office. With it he could command armies, levy taxes, humble his enemies. Although his posture was erect, the King fiddled with a small gold ring set with a ruby on one of the smaller fingers of his right hand. It was worn over the glove. To a more observant eye than Rutter's, this was a nervous tick that betrayed the King's anxiety regarding the mission in crossing the Thames that night.

Rutter snorted. What was royal fashion to him? A small muscular figure, he just pulled the oars. He owned the boat and could already taste the silver from this trip. He had been hired through a servant from the Palace. Did they think he was simple? Even disguised, Rutter knew his passengers now. The King's profile or his late brother's stared back from every coin he'd every collected. But although royals sometimes took the night boat over the pitch-black water, they were usually the young ones. Them in search of some earthy pleasure, thought Rutter. This was different, something was afoot.

The King stood. Rutter eased his stroke to compensate as the boat pitched. The last thing Rutter needed was royalty falling into the Thames. He watched as James II held his balance. The King turned his attention from the object in his hand. It shone in the moonlight.

Rutter wrenched his eyes from it and met the King's stare. He should have looked away, but the King's grim expression held him. The King nodded slowly to him. Rutter, not one for royalty generally, nodded back, before averting his eyes, cursing himself. He was for it now.

The Great Seal dropped into the dark water. Rutter wasn't sure afterwards if he had heard or saw it fall. But it was gone. Forever.

LONDON
1971

CHAPTER 1

THE COUPLE HAD BEEN ARGUING SINCE they'd climbed into the cab; an anniversary dinner turned sour. They were sitting apart. The woman stared out of the window. The man glanced across, not really wanting to make eye contact.

Eyes watched in the driver's mirror. Listening eyes.

The eyes belonged to Tony Pinner; tired, watchful eyes out of place with the well-built frame. As he turned the wheel, Pinner studied the unhappy pair in the mirror. It was a scene he was familiar with. The woman, touching 40, still trim, but tired around the mouth. For too long, it had been set in a thin contemptuous line. The object of her distain was slumped away from her. He was a similar age, but going to seed; hair thinning, waist expanding, slowly becoming an established armchair athlete.

They both work, thought Pinner. Crossing like the tide at breakfast and for the evening meal; a 12-hour cycle. Both busy building careers on sand. Was there room for kids? Pinner cleared his head. It didn't do to dwell on that.

The West End to Muswell Hill was a good hire. So don't knock it, thought Pinner. He settled back into the cold silence of the warring couple and drove. It was what he did.

Approaching City Road, Pinner spotted a fare, a businessman, and turned the wheel to cut across the traffic. The City, the Square Mile, was always full of fares, by day, at least. Mainly short hops; meeting to lunch, lunch to meeting. Pinner pushed aside his half-eaten Caramac bar and drew up at the flagging fare.

"Where to, sir?"

"Clerkenwell Close. OK?"

It was OK with Pinner. A short hop. The fare was either unfamiliar with London's streets and ways, or running late.

Pinner's cab was older than most of those now working the streets – a distinct relic; but well maintained, with an air of romance. It was a rarity; comfortably worn brown leather seats and a sparse functional dashboard in the driver's cockpit. A distinctive and distinguished Austin FX3.

It had been his father's cab. Harold claimed it was the last FX3 in service in London, but Pinner knew better.

There were two others in action to his knowledge; some bloke near Acton, and another one down in Barnes. Two years ago, he had passed one of them on Kensington High Street and the other driver had tooted at him incessantly.

The speedometer almost ticked like a clock; it read miles per hour for minutes.

It had been his dad's second cab. It had rolled off the Carbodies' production line in 1952.

Pinner tended it like a first-born. A regular weekly wax. He took better care of it than he did himself. Or his family – the accusation still stung. One of Olympia's more imaginative barbs. One that had stuck and burrowed deeper.

The FX3 moved among a sea of the newer, more fashionable FX4 models. Pinner had nothing against the new design, he just loved his cab, despite the work it took to keep it on the road. It made him think of his grandfather and that, as always, was a good thing.

Pinner leaned across to get a better look at the fare: in finance, down in the City for a meeting. Perspiring already.

Pinner switched off the FOR HIRE sign and gently turned the wheel. Like most seasoned cabbies, Pinner had that uncanny knack of watching the road and his charge. The man looked slightly creased. It was a big meeting, then.

"Down for the day, sir?"

The man jolted, then brushed at hair he didn't have. His voice was deep, substantial, at odds with the worn slightly pampered look, although his shoes were newly polished. Pinner always noticed people's shoes. You could

5

tell a lot about a man by his shoes. It was something his mum always reckoned.

"Yes, yes. For a meeting."

"She's a big place. People call her the Big Smoke, but a mate of mine calls her the Big Joke."

The man nodded, but failed to hold Pinner's gaze in the mirror. Pinner spotted a gap and glided his cab through, signalling his thanks to another driver.

"It's quite an important meeting," explained the ride, "senior management, budgets and all that."

Pinner nodded sagely. And you're the bacon, summoned to head office to hear the news. There'd been a lot of it recently. Cost cutting. That and industrial disputes. Pinner didn't pay much heed to it while his fare plainly did. The man kept looking at his watch, as though he didn't have much time left.

Pinner pulled the cab over at the corner of Clerkenwell Close and his fare climbed out, shuffling for change and a small tip. Even a condemned man retained his manners.

"Thank you and good luck, sir!"

The man finally met Pinner's gaze and took in the cabbie's meaning. He hesitated as if he wanted to offer something in return, but the moment had passed.

As the FOR HIRE sign flicked on, Pinner looked back in his wing mirror. The fare was standing transfixed in front of the rising building he had come to enter. Another corporate morsel, thought Pinner ruefully.

The FX3 growled along deserted streets. Despite the glare from advertising boards, the night light had a yellow pallor; London with jaundice. Pinner's lone black cab turned onto Tower Bridge. A lane of the bridge was closed for repairs.

They always seemed to be working on it. London Bridge is falling down. Wrong bridge, admitted Pinner. Pinner's cab skirted the repair work. Pinner slowed to inspect the work; a perpetual painting job. Pinner was heading north and then east. Behind him, London was a map of lights. This was his time; this and the dawn.

Pinner ran over the street names like a litany: up Mansell Street, Whitechapel, before swinging left into Cambridge Heath, on to Roman Road, up Globe, before arcing into Gawber Street.

His cab knew the route. Neither cab nor the driver rushed this last part of the journey.

To Gawber Street. For Pinner, the name was enough. But the street had more to offer, 40 years ago, some municipal workmen had seen fit to plant trees periodically along the slightly curved length of the road. It made parking more difficult, but it gave the small line of red brick terraced houses a more genteel air. With that, Gawber Street had come up in the world.

Pinner eased the FX3 up and parked. He did this smoothly, edging up to within two feet of a dirty, battered, red Mini. He loved his cab and the condition of the Mini infuriated him. He switched off the ignition and the cab purred to sleep. Pinner got out, carefully locking the door, his takings muffled in his leather jacket. He paused outside, dragging a dustbin off the kerb. The air was crisp. Frost pending.

Pinner's house was a small Victorian terrace. Built for workers. The doors gave the houses their individual air; like girls in uniform with splashes of different coloured lipsticks.

The front door opened, spilling streetlight onto the polished wooden floor, as Pinner stepped into the hallway. His hand hovered over the light, but he didn't flick the switch.

Stepping quietly into the lounge, he tugged off his battered leather jacket. The room was lit by the lights of London falling into it.

He hung the jacket over a dining chair, checked the silent house quickly and climbed up the stairs. On the landing, he paused to look in on his son Anthony: dark skin even in the shadows and thick, black unruly hair. The boy was sound asleep, an Action Man dangling from the crook of his arm. Pinner smiled.

Pinner turned and quietly entered another room. It was pitch black. He discarded his clothes and climbed into bed. His welcome was a sleepy murmur. Pinner reached across, but only for the warm body to move away from his touch.

Taking a slow breath, Pinner stared up at the ceiling.

"Hello and good night."

CHAPTER 2

A HORSE'S BRIDLE. HOT, RANCID BREATH *steamed out of its nostrils.*
A horse-drawn cab pulled up outside the pub. A gentleman emerged with a painted woman on his arm. Sitting atop the carriage, the hunched cabbie noted the gent and prostitute.

The girl, bloodied and battered, was dead on the cobbles. A gentleman with a cane retreated past a sign which read 'Fournier Street', as a cabbie drew up at the other end of the street. Footsteps echoed down the narrow street.

Pinner had always dreamed of London. They had started when he was a small boy. Cabbies' dreams his mother had called them to coax him off to sleep.

He awoke with the echo of the footsteps running away

from him. Recently, though, the images were becoming increasingly menacing.

Later, as he shaved, the image of the girl's twisted body revisited him and nicked himself. Dark, slow blood ran down his neck, charting a thin map line.

Pinner drove through quiet streets, the early morning light on his face. London was waking up. There was not that much traffic, mainly cabs and buses; red on black.

The capital was an early morning oyster; deliveries being made, traders opening up their small coffee-scented sandwich bars.

Pinner's cab arched into Ladbroke Grove. A tall slim man in an ill-fitting jacket raised his hand. It was a tentative hailing, an apology of sorts, Pinner nodded towards the fare. He's running late again, thought Pinner, as he angled the cab towards the man's spare, round-shouldered frame.

Howard Crosse peered in and nodded in grateful recognition. Pinner smiled and Crosse returned it, almost in relief, and climbed in.

Pinner swung the cab round in a smooth arc in the street. A respectful salute to the double-decker forced to wait while he did so.

"Long day ahead, Mr Crosse?"

Crosse blinked. He was one of life's blinkers.

"Yes. Every day."

Pinner studied the tired man, folded in the back of his cab, his jacket wrapped around him.

"That's the modern world." It was a line his dad used.

His passenger nodded, then shook off his preoccupation. "You?"

"My boy's got a game tonight. Then I'll be out again."

Crosse sighed. "The modern world."

Pinner smiled.

"Pounds, shillings and pence."

Crosse nodded, but he looked distracted. Pinner tried again.

"How's tricks otherwise…" Pinner broke off to beat the lights. The traffic was thickening along Notting Hill Gate as they headed towards London's beating heart.

Crosse came out of his reverie.

"Status Quo."

Pinner laughed.

"Now they're a good band. Stood the test of time."

Crosse leaned forward.

"Still miss it?"

Pinner half laughed, caught out.

"No. Yeah. Good times. She misses it more than I do."

Crosse nodded, but appeared unconvinced. The conversation fell away. Park Lane. Pinner loved London's parks; Victorian keepsakes. His granddad had taken him to them all as a boy. His favourite was Regent's Park. They would stand and listen to the hustings at Speakers' Corner at Hyde Park. There were the regulars, men with well-educated voices, but few means; Communists, Socialists, and Trotskyites pitted against those lamenting the fall of an Empire. Sometimes a leading politician would turn up, just for the fun of it. Pinner doubted that happened today. Too busy mopping up their lunches, thought Pinner. He'd ferried enough of them to have a view on the subject. Still, they put meat on his plate.

Pinner made a decision and cut across to take the cab right, away from the main flow south.

Pinner studied Crosse, but his fare's mind was elsewhere. Pinner respected his silence. A cabbie had to know when to be quiet.

Crosse pointed ahead as they approached St James's Park.

"If you could just…"

Pinner understood. He knew about the rear entrance to Downing Street; it was not a well-kept secret.

"You'll walk the rest." Crosse was a creature of habit. Aren't we all, thought Pinner.

Crosse nodded. From the edge of his seat, he craned forward.

"Eleven, alright with you?"

Pinner had his eye on the traffic; still slow for this time of day. Not many cabs out either. But he was listening.

"Yeah. Horse Guards. The daily grind."

Crosse climbed out.

"Thanks, Tony." Crosse waved the money at the cabbie. Pinner took it politely.

"Mr Crosse."

Crosse walked off. A few moments passed. Pinner always allowed himself a sliver of time between each fare. A small ritual. He checked the fare, added the running total to his take for the day; scanned the back seat to make sure Mr Crosse hadn't left anything behind – only his air of anxiety. What did he have to be worried about, thought Pinner.

Crosse was one of Pinner's regular fares. Pinner had first picked him up about four years ago. A thin man with a slight stoop, drenched after missing his bus. Months later, he'd climbed into Pinner's cab again. That day, it was outside Mansion House, in a dinner jacket that had probably never fitted him; bunking off early from some City social.

The FOR HIRE sign flicked on again. Pinner's cab edged out as Big Ben read 7.45am.

Pinner's cab turned into Whitehall. Slowly he drove past as Crosse was showing his pass at the entrance to Downing Street.

Crosse usually took the back entrance. It was his habit. Not today, thought Pinner. The change made him uneasy. Perhaps it wasn't going to be a good day after all. Pinner changed gear and pushed the thought aside.

A black cab, a shiny new FX4, was parked outside a gentleman's club. A figure in a dark frockcoat emerged, face obscured by the collar. The cabbie quickly got out of the cab and opened the door for the man.

Big Frank, the club doorman, was watching and frowning slightly at the same time. He'd encountered these two before. The driver had a slight Latin look. But there was nothing romantic about him, admitted Frank. People called him Angel. Perhaps it was a joke of some sort. Frank had made enquiries about him and the other one, Morden. He hadn't got far. Not to be crossed, not even by Big Frank and that was saying something. Frank had seen it before. The smaller one, he was the worry; a queer one, but a killer. Frank wouldn't be surprised if he carried a knife or worse. The pair made Frank uneasy. Although he wouldn't admit the root of his unease, it was there; fear.

Frank watched the cab drive off. Good riddance to 'em, he thought.

Olympia's was a traditional London café in need of a lick of paint, lodged at a quiet junction near a railway arch not far from Bethnal Green. A grand name for a tired joint.

An assortment of black cab models was parked up like suitors on kerbs nearby, when Pinner's cab drew up.

As he entered the small, dated café, Pinner was wrapped in a battered old leather jacket; a dark urban cloak for the city.

The café was a bizarre mix: Formica tabletops and school chairs with black and white tiled flooring. Large posters of Blues and Jazz singers and musicians formed exotic blocks of colour. It had once been a corner shop, the kind of place your mum or granny would have sent you to get something she'd forgotten. Pinner felt he could almost remember it as a shop. Maybe he was fooling himself.

The café had a warm, busy atmosphere that was a contrast to the furniture's sparseness. A couple of groups of men were sipping from large mugs, or rustling papers as Pinner stepped in. One or two of the men acknowledged him, as Pinner made his way to a window table. One of the chairs at the small square table was already taken.

Toby Kensal, a hefty man, slightly past his prime, was reading a paper. Studying the racing pages, he was wearing a three-piece suit. Kensal, even when he looked out of place, had that knack of fitting in. He was the kind of man often described as a character, especially by those who disliked his manner and there were plenty of them.

The only woman in the place was also the only person working. Vicki was in her twenties, slim and tired.

Kensal looked up sensing Pinner's arrival.

"Vicki! A mug for my mate!"

Vicki put a hand on her hip.

"He's already got one."

Pinner smiled at her, while Kensal pretended he hadn't got the joke. Vicky moved to get the order as Pinner pulled off his jacket and sat opposite his friend.

"Rough night?"

Pinner gave a tired nod.

Kensal turned back towards Vicki.

"A couple of bacon rolls as well, Vick."

Vicky looked a mite exasperated, but gave Pinner a resigned smile. Looking at the back of Kensal's head, she stuck her tongue out in his direction, but it was a discreet act of defiance.

Kensal folded away his paper and his chances of winning.

"How's tricks?"

Vicki placed the steaming mug in front of Pinner.

He smiled at her.

"Thanks."

Pinner nodded to Kensal

"Cheers."

Kensal stared straight back.

"Up yours."

They both smiled.

Back at the hotplate, Vicki turned over the bacon and reached for the red and brown sauces.

Pinner indicated Kensal's racing pages; Wimbledon and Catford dog tracks. Kensal had always preferred them to the nags, betting for the common man, he called it.

"Any form?"

Kensal shrugged.

"Been cleared out. Need a new accountant." Kensal shifted his bulk.

Pinner could see his point.

"Pounds, shillings and pence."

Pinner glanced at his watch, but Kensal spotted him.

"Forgot. Almost time for your regular date," Kensal snorted in derision, but Pinner just shrugged.

"Still on for today, is it?"

Pinner smiled and studied his watch again.

"Yeah. Meeting ends at 11."

Kensal did the same. His watch was gold and small for such a big man.

"Plenty time, then."

The cough of an engine buffeted the large front window of the café. It was more of a choke that caused Vicki to look up. A rider on a scooter, with a clipboard on the front windscreen jumped up on to the kerb outside the café; a struggling Knowledge Boy.

All black cab drivers had to acquire The Knowledge, a test to earn their prized badge. It could take years to learn more than 300 runs, all within a six-mile radius of Trafalgar Square that marked the centre of the capital; the streets, attractions, history, road systems.

It had taken Pinner just two years, but he had started young, his grandfather had begun testing him when he was still in short trousers.

Kensal gave a sad shake of his head.

"Here comes the Boy Blunder."

The rider kept his helmet on and ambled into the café.

"Get that helmet off! No robbers allowed." Vicki pointed at him.

The sparse figure in an old combat jacket and faded jeans pulled off his helmet. Preston was a young Scot with a lop-sided grin and lank flaxen fair. On his lapel was a small pin badge of Che Guevara.

He walked over and kissed Vicki, before turning to Pinner and Kensal. She, at least, was pleased to see him.

"Guys." A flat-handed acknowledgement.

Kensal grunted dismissively, although Pinner nodded a small greeting. Preston pulled up a chair, like a lanky cowboy joining a card game in a saloon.

Kensal shifted his weight.

"Alright, let's get this over with. Where were you last night?"

Preston gathered himself for the trial ahead, eyes flickering between the two experienced cab drivers. Pinner had been a cabbie for less than ten years, but Kensal, well, Preston suspected he thought he'd been a cabbie before the wheel had been invented. It was the main reason he dreaded these ritualistic examinations.

"Right. Yeah. Walthamstow Dogs to the British Museum."

"Straightforward enough."

Kensal looked across at Pinner for confirmation. Pinner nodded slightly.

"Alright, let's hear it."

Preston took a breath of courage. A squire faced by two seasoned knights.

"Right. Turn left into Chingford Road, on to Forrest Road, Ferry Lane, Broad Lane, Seven Sisters. That becomes Parkhurst, then Camden. Then turn off at Camden Street and down into Eversholt. It's marginally quieter at that time of night."

Vicki put down the bacon rolls. Kensal indicated the same for Preston.

"Right at Euston Road, traffic lights out."

He looked up for encouragement and Pinner rewarded him with a nod.

"Left into Gordon Street, there's a square there, before Russell Square, then Montague."

Vicki was at Preston's shoulder.

"Bedford, Montague is the next one."

Vicki put Preston's breakfast in front of him. Preston looked flummoxed, but Vicki nodded encouragingly.

Preston recovered his train of thought.

"Aye, right, I mean left into Bedford and I'm outside the museum. On Russell Street."

Vicki gave Preston a kiss, a smile and turned away. Preston was grinning, mainly with relief, but Kensal was shaking his head. He stabbed his fat finger at Preston.

"She ought to be doing this not you. A walking compass that's what she is."

Preston's gaze was still on Vicki.

"Some walk."

Kensal dismissed the youthful innuendo.

"Keep your mind on the route, son. Next time, remember the one-way street."

That deflated Preston, who mentally began to go over his run again, shaking his head slightly as Kensal's point made sense. He had overlooked it. While he struggled over the routes he had to memorize, Vicki could recall them at will.

He had always thought he had a good memory. Up until six months ago, he had been a student, until he had been challenged one night on being a Scot in London; someone who could never really know or understand the city.

Preston's response had been radical.

He had jacked in his university course and enrolled as a Knowledge Boy. He was determined to become a black cab driver.

He glanced at the tired scooter parked outside and felt his resolve stiffening. One day it would be a cab.

The door opened and a stunningly beautiful woman, Olympia, swept in to the café. Vicki smiled at her in greeting.

Olympia took off her coat and started pulling on an apron. Vicki nodded towards Pinner who looked across the café at the striking new arrival. Olympia and Pinner exchanged crooked smiles. The kind shared by people who knew each other too well and whose conversations felt increasingly rehearsed.

Olympia nodded at the other men and started clearing Pinner and Kensal's table.

Kensal sat back, although his voice still carried; just enough for everyone in the café to hear.

"Love is all around us."

Olympia ignored Kensal, her words were for Pinner.

"Don't forget; 4pm for Anthony."

Pinner nodded. Olympia headed behind the counter, her message delivered.

Pinner rose reluctantly. He needed to get out of the café. Kensal raised an eyebrow.

"You done?"

Pinner looked down on him.

"I'm done."

Pinner picked up his jacket, acknowledged Olympia and headed for the door. Kensal leaned forward to make his point.

"I mean you have been, mate."

Pinner didn't reply, but checked at the door and looked across at Olympia, who stopped putting change into the till and looked up.

Pinner looked back at her.

"Good morning and goodbye."

Olympia studied him and ignored the anxious look of Vicki and the studied expression on Kensal's face. Preston and Vicki shared a look, as Pinner walked slowly towards his cab.

Preston and Kensal watched him from the café window through a curtain of condensation.

"He looks rough." Preston kept his voice low.

Kensal grunted.

"Eat your breakfast. One day you'll have a mortgage."

Kensal took a mouth of tea. He savoured it, before the punchline.

"If you live that long." Kensal looked back towards Pinner, as his friend climbed into his cab.

Pinner was driving, he glanced at his watch: 11.00am dead. Pinner looked ahead judging the traffic on Victoria Street 100 yards ahead. He could see a small crowd with hoisted banners. A cluster of postal workers picketing the wide pavement in front of the Post Office with police officers standing nearby. The first national postal strike, Pinner had read. He knew a few of them, those on strike. He had sat in The Crown with them, while Kensal had berated the posties for being unpatriotic. Kensal didn't hold with strikes. Then, Kensal didn't hold with much.

He slowed down as the pickets spilled onto the road, while a tired-looking police officer tried to keep the traffic moving.

He hated being late. He hoped Crosse's meeting had over-run. That would be a first, he thought.

Horse Guards was busy. Crosse, his grey raincoat buttoned up and clutching a battered brown briefcase, was searching up and down the street. Crosse looked at his watch for a third time, made a decision and stepped forward to hail a cab, any cab.

Pinner spotted his fare 50 yards up Whitehall, glanced in his mirror and moved his cab across towards Crosse. Late, but he had made it.

The growl of an engine gunning caught Pinner's attention.

As he glanced to his left, another black cab cut right across Pinner's, blocking him off. Pinner slammed down his brake, anger flashing across Pinner's face.

"What the hell…"

Pinner turned the wheel, still determined to reach Crosse. The other cab angled further across to block him. It was almost as if it was deliberate.

As Pinner watched, a second cab moved across and stopped in front of Crosse.

Pinner was now completely hemmed in.

Pinner tooted his horn in anger and frustration.

At the blurt of the horn, Crosse looked across at Pinner's cab. Pinner could see his long, pale face.

The fare looked confused, hesitant. Pinner watched as the driver of the other cab leaned across the seat indicating for Crosse to hurry up and get in. Almost reluctantly, Crosse climbed in.

Pinner exhaled slowly, as he watched the other cab, number plate SE1 6NJ, drive off.

"Wanker!"

Pinner fingered his wedding ring.

Pinner's gaze moved from the cab which had picked up Crosse to the one that cut him off: SE1 6NJ and SE1 2PY. Pinner frowned. A chance in a million. Unlike his friend Kensal, Pinner was not a betting man.

CHAPTER 3

*F*LAMES ENGULFING A CAB; A CHARCOAL *frame against a red-hot surround. Bombs falling and sirens wailing. A section of wall pitching forward, leaving a home sheared like a giant doll's house, its rooms exposed to the Blitz. Another cab, piled with firemen spinning around the rubble as an explosion rocked the street. Dust, smoke and death.*

Pinner's cab was sitting in a rank. He awoke as a young couple, slightly unsteady on their feet approached the cab. Pinner struggled to drag himself out of his dark dream as the couple climbed in. He rarely fell asleep in his cab and chided himself for doing so.

The man and woman were in drunken good humour. She leaned against him in the back seat.

Pinner looked back.

"Where you after, sir?"

The young man didn't even look up.

"Just get us to bloody Dalston, Mate, alright."

Pinner's eyes narrowed in the central mirror.

"Another word like that and you'll be out on your ear. Savvy?"

The man looked surprised. The woman giggled.

"Cool it, man, it's only bloody Dalston," the emphasis was a challenge.

Pinner's eyes in the mirror fixed on the passenger, drunk on love and youth. The ignition was abruptly turned off.

Pinner, still in his dated leather jacket, climbed out of his cab. He swung open the passenger door and hauled the man out. Shock washed the other man's face as he was sent sprawling onto the pavement. He looked up at Pinner, who stared back – ready. Pinner turned to the woman passenger. He smiled and inclined his head indicating that she should step out of his cab. Uncertain and uneasy, she did so.

Pinner nodded to her and climbed back into his cab, then switched on the FOR HIRE sign.

As the FOR HIRE sign went on Pinner's cab drove off.

The Crown was comfortably busy with shift workers; off-duty police officers, postmen and taxi drivers. The Crown was a bar in rebellion against modernisation. High ceilings, yellowed with age, tobacco and gossip. Cut-glass chandeliers that defused the light down on to a square bar set against one wall. No women; The Crown had yet to recognise the Suffragette movement.

Rounded steel columns kept The Crown standing no matter how many you had. Drunkenness was rare here; this was a port for those who worked against the clock, toiling while the majority of the capital were still in bed.

The talk was of last Saturday's match, this Saturday's game and rising fuel prices. West Ham on their uppers, Arsenal flying high. Smoke settled in a layer at head height.

Kensal, in a loud suit, a shiny 1950s relic, was sitting with a paper and his pint when Pinner walked in. Kensal seemed to wear a different suit every day, a lifetime of fittings from Lipman's on Charing Cross Road. One suit a year since he'd married and he had kept every one. They all got an airing.

Kensal, picking him out, waved an arm in salute. The barman, Maurice, knew what to pour.

"Alright, Tone."

"Yeah. Alright, Maurice. Thanks."

Pinner carried the pints over to Kensal.

Kensal detected Pinner's mood.

"You look happy."

Pinner took a sip of his beer. Kensal waited.

"Got cut up. Some Jack on Whitehall. It was blatant. SE bloody one."

"Thought you said it was Whitehall."

"It was. The bloody plate on the cab."

Kensal shrugged, it was all beer to him.

"Forget it, mate. Ain't worth it."

Kensal shifted his bulk.

"Plain or salt 'n ' vinegar?"

Pinner shook his head.

"Please yourself," as Kensal headed back to the bar. While Pinner took another mouthful of his pint, he looked around the pub. The posties were in a large ring. Someone was retiring. Perhaps being on strike was thirsty work. Good luck to them. The coppers sat in smaller bands. This was not a time for mixing; the picket line divide had crossed into The Crown.

He looked across at the bar to where Kensal and another man, a compact athletic figure, were talking in low, hurried voices. Pinner frowned. The voices were tense, the words indistinct.

Kensal appeared to be in bother. Pinner did not recognise the other man; an offended postal worker perhaps, as Kensal was forthright in his condemnation of public servants withdrawing their labour. For Kensal, it was unpatriotic, if not a form of minor Treason.

Pinner rose. As he approached, Maurice moved along the bar, almost shadowing him. Kensal turned as if he could sense his friend's intent. The man, too, turned to face Pinner. He had a face ready for a fight. He sneered at Pinner's ageing leather jacket and snorted in quiet derision.

If Maurice looked concerned, so did Kensal as he turned to place himself between Pinner and his foe.

"Just a bit of banter, Tone. Me and Alan, here."

Pinner's eyes were fixed on Alan. They were measuring each other, causing Kensal and Maurice to exchange a quick, worried glance.

"Salt and vinegar. All Maurice had."

Kensal eased Pinner away, a placating palm on his arm.

Pinner allowed himself to be guided back to his seat, but he was still looking at Alan, who was studying him in return.

The pair sat down, Pinner with a hint of reluctance.

"Christ, Tone. Just a bit of banter that went awry," Kensal was babbling slightly, however, Pinner was still watching Alan, who turned slowly back to the bar and ordered from a plainly relieved Maurice.

"Here, have a crisp. You can't afford any more bother. You know that."

Pinner's stately cab drew up outside his well-kept terrace house and he climbed out. Pinner rested his hands on the roof. Olympia's unloved Mini was abandoned rather than parked, one wheel on the kerb. The Austin was so much more impressive than the property, he thought. Abruptly, he turned and climbed back into the cab, turned on the ignition and moved off.

Beth Pinner, a small, thin woman, was ironing in her tiny kitchen. She was singing along quietly to a song on the radio; Mario Lanza. The kitchen was from a different era; a marriage of 1940s post-war austerity and comfort.

The scrape of a key in the door alerted her to her son's visit, but Beth kept ironing when Pinner filled the doorway.

"How many more times do I have to tell you, mum? It's not safe. You gotta keep it locked."

Beth pursed her lips.

"I know where you've been. Can tell by your humour. If you want to be useful, put the kettle on."

"Is that him? Is that you, Tone?" The voice was worn and strained, as if struggling to make it through from the living room.

Beth indicated that Pinner should go through to the other room, as she moved to take the kettle from her son.

"I'll see to that. Ask him if he wants a biscuit."

Tony walked through into the sitting room. It was tidy and unassuming, characteristics it shared with Pinner's parents. Harold Pinner, a pale shell of a man, was sitting in an armchair. He looked drawn and unhealthy, but pleased to see his son.

"Hi, dad. How you doing?"

They clasped hands briefly; old and young. Pinner found himself studying the thin, blue veins and pale liver spots on his father's hands.

Harold spoke with an effort and a wheeze.

"Better than she thinks," Harold jerked his head towards the kitchen door. A conspiracy quickly established between father and son.

Harold broke down coughing violently. The attempt at humour had proved too taxing. Pinner looked at his dad's frail frame.

On the mantelpiece was a picture of a band of musicians; a beautiful young singer, Olympia, and her band behind her. Her gaze was torn between the camera and one of the band members – a young, smiling Tony Pinner.

Pinner turned away from the picture. He wished his mum would just bin it, but he knew from experience, Beth never let anything go.

Beth was stacking dirty mugs. Pinner was tapping the barometer on the wall. It was a habit he had inherited from his dad.

"So, Sunday's OK."

Pinner nodded, only half-listening.

"No sudden cancellations, Tony. We haven't seen Ant since his birthday," Beth's tone changed.

"Yeah. See you later, mum, say goodbye to dad for me."

Howard had fallen asleep midway through their cup of tea. He spent his days drifting off.

Beth bit her lip and impulsively gave Pinner a hug. He turned away, embarrassed. As Pinner reached the door, Beth made her point. She had no qualms about shooting someone as they retreated.

"Spoke to Olympia yesterday. She said Sunday would be fine."

Pinner, caught out, checked for a moment, then left without answering. The hacking pain of Harold coughing his guts up saw him out.

As Pinner drove, he glanced back at the female passenger and her two children. The mum was shattered, her kids listless, obviously tired faces, framed by shopping bags. Welcome to the real world, thought Pinner, all choice and no options. Pounds, shillings and pence.

He pulled up outside Olympia's Café. Although still open, some of the chairs had been piled onto tables, making it seem even more like a small classroom.

When Pinner walked in, Vicki was cleaning up. She smiled at him. Her smile was one of the reasons he had given her the job.

"It's OK, Vicki."

Pinner poured himself a large mug of tea from a bulbous metal tea pot. He emptied the till's takings and carried the mug and the day's takings to a table. Pinner laid the cash out and started to count it. Usually, Pinner enjoyed this time. The café ticked over. Yeah, ticked over, that summed everything up, he thought, as he reached for his tea.

From the small radio, George Harrison called quietly on 'My Sweet Lord'. Harrison, the quiet one of the quartet, was the only Beatle that Pinner really rated.

The stuttering of Preston's scooter intruded on his counting. Pinner looked up to confirm the Scot's arrival.

Preston walked in, nodded at Pinner, then walked up and gave Vicki a kiss. Vicki brushed him off with a kind laugh and started to pour tea.

"No, thanks, I'll just annoy Tony."

Pinner looked up as Preston joined him. He put his rucksack and clipboard down. Pinner raised an eyebrow, but Preston just shrugged.

"Maybe I should have stuck at Law."

"Each to their own."

"Like you and Olympia."

Pinner focused on Preston.

"Vicki says Olympia used to be in a band."

Preston nodded at all the posters. One of them announced 'The Peppers'. Olympia's face stared out at them; younger and happier.

Pinner came out of his reverie and looked hard at Preston.

"Yeah."

Preston waited and, after a breath, Pinner relented. Another man's patience makes you do that.

"Great voice. Jazz, Blues."

"You?"

"Second rate bass," Pinner shrugged.

"But you got the girl."

With that, Pinner saw Preston properly for the first time. "Yeah." Maybe Preston would have made a good lawyer.

As Pinner locked the café's angled door, he turned to watch the young couple giggling as they climbed aboard Preston's ancient scooter. He'd paid too much for it from a garage near Mile End. Kensal had given him another earful for that misjudgement. Preston, with Vicki riding pillion, headed off. They both waved and Pinner returned the goodbye.

"I got the girl."

The words felt strange, but so was the sentiment. Or maybe just stale and forgotten.

CHAPTER 4

Pinner's cab was parked up outside Globe Primary School. At the school gate, Olympia was fussing over Anthony and his tie. She passed him his bag. The boy took it, then stepped up onto the luggage plate and reached through the front side window for Pinner and his son to clasp hands. Anthony turned back and hugged his mother.

Olympia stepped back into the cab, as Anthony joined the current of pupils streaming into the schoolyard. Another quick, shy wave, and he was gone.

Pinner turned from watching his son to look at his wife in the mirror. He started to smile. Olympia caught him and frowned.

They drove to the café in a silence magnified by the sound of the traffic.

As Olympia climbed out, she hesitated, as if she was

going to say something or perhaps even give Pinner a kiss. But she did neither.

Pinner watched her walk into the café.

"Hello and goodbye."

Pinner shook his head in tired resignation and spun the wheel.

Pinner flicked on the FOR HIRE sign and turned his thoughts to safer ground.

The Strand. Pinner's cab edged across the traffic to pick up a fare. They were a middle-aged couple; tourists, their hands clutching a limp London A-Z.

Pinner flicked the indicator. Normally, he'd relish this; a chance to flash his knowledge of the capital, the standard history book stuff that everyone used to learn at school interlaced with darker, more sinister, histories. Like his dreams. Today, he would rather just drive, so he did.

Tourists loved the fact that his cab was older, more established. For them, it was like stepping back into history.

True, the luggage sometimes got a bit damp, but Pinner felt that was a small inconvenience. As his grandfather used to say: History has a price.

The couple were pointing out at the landmarks even before they got into his cab. Pinner looked back and smiled at their enthusiasm. Sometimes Pinner played the tour guide, giving them a bright smile and the benefit of his studies; dark tales of murder in narrow alleys, or sometimes a bit of royal gossip. They usually lapped it up. But this couple were very self-contained. After a while you got a sense for it. They knew exactly what they wanted to see and Pinner knew when to keep mum. Careless talk costs lives, that's it. It was another of his granddad's stock maxims.

They were Belgium. Not quite French. Pinner smiled in spite of himself. Hearing his granddad's voice say it.

Pinner was watching the traffic lights ahead. His meter accumulating steadily, shillings and pence. That was a job to get done, to change the meter before the changeover, he reminded himself. Though he resented any change imposed on his prized cab.

He glanced across at a tired-looking newspaper seller. The old man was holding up a London Evening Standard. Not the paper it once was, thought Pinner. His mum still bought it. So did he, if he was counting.

Today he would read it, because Howard Crosse's face stared back at Pinner from the front page.

The lights changed to green as Pinner slammed on the brakes. The tourists in the back were thrown from their seats, buffeted by Flemish oaths.

Throwing open his door, Pinner raced around the front of his cab. Other cars and taxis were hooting at him as they slammed on their brakes.

Reaching the newspaper seller, Pinner thrust money at the old man. In his hands, the headline screamed at him:

BODY FOUND IN THAMES.

The café door was pushed open and Kensal shuffled into Olympia's. Like many big men, Kensal was light on his feet; nimble, armed with a paper in his hand. He waved it like a short sword. "Morning all."

He located Olympia behind the counter.

"The usual, darling."

Olympia gave a tired nod and raised an eyebrow at Vicki. Both women had developed a long-term tolerance to Kensal, his jokes and blatant lack of sensitivity.

The café was busy. Mornings were their best time. Olympia and Vicki worked well together; banter across the counter, problems shared, halved and put aside.

Kensal sat heavily in his usual perch and rustled his paper when the door burst open. Framed in the doorway, Pinner stood like a gunfighter brandishing a rolled up newspaper of his own.

The entire café stared at him. Pinner looked from Olympia to Kensal. He strode forward and slammed the paper down in front of Kensal.

Kensal and Crosse faced each other.

Kensal gently took the paper from his friend. Olympia strained over Kensal's shoulder to see the missing man's face.

Kensal scanned the report.

"That's him, SE1, that's what I was telling you about."

Kensal, deliberating, took his time, pulling out small circular reading spectacles. Somewhat gingerly, he started to read aloud as though to small children.

"Police have confirmed that the body is that of Howard Crosse, a high-ranking Civil Servant. The 54-year-old Government Official had not been seen since Thursday morning at 11am after a meeting in Whitehall."

"Thursday morning. That's him. That's when I saw him. My regular date."

Pinner turned to Kensal and Olympia.

"The 11 o'clock man," then Olympia realised who Pinner meant. Kensal looked doubtful.

"You're sure, Tone?"

Pinner nodded, definite.

"SE1."

Olympia frowned.

"What?"

Pinner turned to her.

"That's the plate on the cab that cut me up. And the one that picked him up."

Kensal turned to Olympia.

"Where's that tea, darling?"

Olympia looked at Kensal blankly.

"It'll help us figure this out. There's a good girl."

Olympia looked annoyed, but turned away to get the tea. Kensal leaned in towards his friend.

"You sure about this?"

"Positive."

Pinner began to pull his jacket on, but Kensal waved the paper at him.

"Hold your horses, mate. Have your tea. Let it settle. Sure you want to get involved? You could be wrong."

Pinner shook his head.

"Alright, what was the rest of the plate? They'll ask you that."

Pinner looked surprised, uncertain, and his frown showed it.

"See, you're not so sure now."

Olympia put mugs and plates in front of them.

"Thanks, darling," but Olympia did not move away. Kensal glanced at her, only Olympia ignored him and concentrated on Pinner's face. Pinner looked between them.

"No, I'll call in at Bow Street."

Pinner looked again between his wife and his friend.

"But, I'll have my breakfast first."

Olympia and Kensal both smiled back at him.

"Two shillings, dahlin'!"

Kensal looked up at Olympia in surprise. Olympia's hand was out, waiting. Pinner could not help his smile. Slowly, with a hint of ill-grace, Kensal handed over the money. Olympia swept the coins up and strutted away.

Pinner was sitting in his cab, the folded newspaper resting in his lap. He looked across at Bow Street Police Station. He gathered himself and opened the cab door.

The reception area was quiet. Pinner stood, hesitating in the doorway. He took a step forward, looked around. Abruptly, he turned and walked out again.

Pinner was driving, heading out east. The cab was empty, but the FOR HIRE sign was switched off. Pinner passed the Tower of London. Now there was a place. It had grown as London had: from fortress, to prison, to garrison, treasure store to tourist attraction. That was history for you.

A police car, a powerful Rover, passed on the other side of the road, Pinner watched it, deep in thought.

As he drove east, he spotted a police officer talking to a man in the street. For a moment, Pinner was back in the police cell; surrounded by four close walls and the reek of urine and carbolic, bruised, angry and ashamed, wondering if the man he had attacked was badly hurt.

He'd survived the experience as his opponent had the beating and, later, the man had refused to press any charges. It had been a lucky escape, otherwise, Pinner would never have been able to become a cabbie. It made him value his badge all the more.

Pinner and Anthony were racing Scalextric cars on a track laid out on the lounge floor, when the front door opened. Today, it was the British Grand Prix.

Olympia slipped her bag off her shoulder.

"Hi."

They both looked up to the doorway and smiled at her, the woman in their life.

"How'd you get on?" Pinner looked at her, but didn't answer, concentrating instead on his son.

"One more race before your tea."

Olympia put her hands into the pockets of her short skirt and watched them, studying the back of Pinner's head. He looked up. She nodded slightly, her suspicions confirmed, and left the room carrying another small disappointment. Pinner's car skidded off the track, sending Anthony's arms aloft in victory.

"Champion!"

Pinner was loitering just inside the police station entrance. The reception area was busy today. Officers were coming on duty, going off. People were perched on benches, waiting. A tired uniformed officer greeted arrivals at the desk. Pinner looked around. He could feel the tension across his shoulders.

He was pushed aside as two officers struggled to direct a figure past him.

The youth's face was twisted in rage.

"Get off me!"

The police officers looked unmoved, nothing they had not heard before. One, mid-struggle, spoke to Pinner.

"Sorry, mate."

The youth was hauled off in a headlock and a painful arm grip.

Pinner reached the desk and was met by an unsmiling, young female officer.

"Yes?"

"Hi, hello. I've come about Howard Crosse. He went missing. I saw him yesterday."

The officer looked at Pinner as if he might be wasting her time.

Pinner put the paper down on the desk between them and pointed at the picture.

"Him. Saw him."

The officer adjusted her bra strap and read the first few paragraphs, then looked up.

"OK. If you won't mind waiting, sir."

Pinner was still waiting impatiently in reception when the same officer appeared at the desk.

"Excuse me. Sir!"

Everyone looked up, so did Pinner.

Then he realised she was signalling him. He rose and walked across reluctantly, conscious of others who were still waiting watching him.

"We don't have anyone who can see you right now. Can you leave your contact details, please? Sorry."

Pinner felt exasperated and relieved at the same time, but wrote out his name, address and telephone number.

When Pinner came out of the station it was raining. As he approached his cab, he checked and picked off a parking ticket. He shook his head in frustration. *Do the right thing.*

Pinner's cab was parked in Grafton Square, a quiet street

north of Clapham Common. He was sitting in the gloom, the lights from the street lamps illuminating him. The paper rested in his lap.

Odd, that a man should die and all the paper reports is the manner of it. What about his wife? Shirley or Cynthia, Pinner seemed to remember. The daughter was called Rebecca. Pinner smiled, remembering Crosse talking about the girl heading off for a gap year, then Oxford University. Following in her father's footsteps. Don't we all, thought Pinner, as he touched the dashboard. From the cradle to the cab to the grave – an alternative Welfare State and an unofficial cabbie's code. Crosse had been his charge and Pinner had failed him.

Olympia was serving customers, busy but in control. She looked up to find Kensal was sitting in his usual perch. Squatting would be a better description, she thought. Strange, she hadn't even heard the door open. As Pinner came in, he looked towards Olympia, but Kensal motioned him over. Olympia straightened to watch the two men, irked that her husband had gone to speak to his friend first. That shouldn't bother her.

Pinner sat down.

"How's tricks, partner?"

Pinner shrugged, looking up. Olympia was standing over them.

She stared down at Pinner with unforgiving purpose.

"Well? Did you see the police?"

Pinner glanced at Kensal.

Kensal raised his palm, a gesture of appeal.

"Hold your horses, Olympia. What's this all about? Some missing accountant."

Olympia dismissed Kensal.

"Do what's right, Tony."

Kensal looked concerned.

"Easy, mate, you and the police – you don't mix."

Pinner looked between them.

"I went this morning."

Olympia and Kensal stared at him; theirs were two very different expressions.

CHAPTER 5

AS DAWN CAME ON, A SLEEK BLACK CAB
pulled up outside Pinner's house.

Leather gloved hands were resting gently on
the wheel. Eyes scanned the street, but there was no sign
of Pinner's cab.

In the back of the cab, another pair of leather gloves
were pulled on to a pair of well-manicured hands.

Pinner trudged to his cab. Light was reaching out over the
houses on the opposite side of the street. The great thing
about the morning was that you owned it, the day was
yours to make or waste, Pinner thought.

As he opened the driver's door, the grate of footsteps
made him pause. Pinner shielded his eyes against the
morning dazzle.

"Tony Pinner?"

"Yeah."

Pinner's eyes adjusted. Morden was a thin-faced man, with short-cropped hair. His shoes were highly polished. The second man was younger, taller, darker, his hair fashionably long, but tied back in a ponytail. It was a bizarre fashion statement, a vanity that gave him a strange exotic menace.

Both wore expensive suits, their cut emphasised by their black leather gloves. Angel's roll neck sweater moulded his muscular frame. Not everyone could carry it off, acknowledged Pinner, surprised by the thought. Morden wore a collar and tie with a Windsor knot – sharp, stylish and costly; looked like Jermyn Street or similar, not commonplace in Gawber Street.

While Morden leaned on the roof of Pinner's cab, Angel stopped a couple of feet away from Pinner. A little too close.

Morden smiled. A crooked uncomfortable expression.

"The Collector sends his regards."

Pinner looked blank, but felt uneasy.

"In fact, he sends a request," Morden paused for effect, "No more talking to the Peelers."

Pinner looked between the two men.

Morden touched his forelock. A mocking gesture.

"With due respect."

Morden patted the roof of Pinner's FX3 almost lovingly.

The two men moved away and climbed into a black cab parked across the road. Pinner watched it drive off, Angel, wearing leather gloves was driving, Morden reclining in the back. Neither man looked back at him.

The cab's number plate read SE1 6QA. Pinner took it in.

Pinner watched them go. He climbed into his cab and studied his reflection in the driver's mirror. He frowned as a long-buried memory stirred.

Pinner pulled up outside Olympia's and climbed out of the cab, but checked at the gunning of another cab. Pinner turned as a cab emerged from the side of the café, with Kensal at the wheel. Pinner raised his hand.

"Toby!"

Kensal looked across at him and raised his arm in acknowledgement, but did not stop. Pinner's arm dropped as Kensal's cab turned into the road.

At the café window, Vicki was watching Pinner standing in middle of the road. Olympia joined her.

The women watched as Pinner walked back to his cab. Olympia reached the door.

"Tony!"

Pinner looked back and waved, but shook his head at the same time. With that, he climbed into his cab and drove off. Olympia watched him go, her message undelivered.

Pinner helped Anthony out of his cab. The boy was in school uniform. The school run was a welcome break from fares and rank queuing for Pinner. He had never resented Olympia's assumption that he should break off from work to meet their son from school and ferry him to football matches. He was enjoying his son being eight. Anthony's relaxed demeanour and the smile he had inherited from his mother, combined with an early talent with a ball at his feet, meant he was popular and his background had not been an issue. At least, not yet for Anthony.

As they approached the front door of the Pinner's terraced house, the next door opened. His neighbour, Alice, smiled at him, her timing and flat delivery were impeccable.

"The police were here earlier."

Pinner stopped and looked straight at her, while Anthony looked up at his dad.

"Just thought I'd pass it on."

Pinner nodded.

"Thanks, Alice. I'll give them a call."

Alice nodded, but looked sceptical.

Kipping's Yard was a garage encircled by columns of old tyres, tucked between a railway line and a council estate. Pinner stood waiting while a mechanic looked at his meter. Every cab in London was making the change. Another cost in preparation for the new coinage.

Images of Crosse and taxi number plates appeared wherever Pinner looked. His reverie was cut short by the blurt of a horn. Pinner turned at the interruption. Kensal was at the wheel of his cab. Like his suits, Kensal's cab was also immaculate. He clambered out, with a rolled up newspaper in his fist. For Kensal, the paper went with the suit. Pinner had never seen him without either. He signalled Pinner as he trudged across avoiding small oil spills.

"Watcha mate."

Pinner nodded at Kensal's cab.

Kensal patted her bonnet with real affection.

"She's getting old. But Eddie'll show the old girl a good time."

Eddie laughed. The mechanic was a grizzled older man, who grinned as he wiped his hands.

"She's fine. Better have a word with Toby's old girl."

"Mine's a young bit of stuff compared to his old Dame," Kensal often feigned impatience and a gentle tolerance with Pinner for keeping the FX3. However, Pinner sensed that Kensal felt differently. That, in fact, he took a perverse pride in his mate's stubborn love affair with the older cab. No turning it in for a younger model for Pinner.

Eddie sauntered past them, a new meter tucked underneath his arm.

Kensal considered his friend.

"You alright, Tone."

"Not sure. Yeah, you know. I'm fine."

Kensal nodded, studying his friend for the underlying cause.

"Toby, you ever heard of The Collector."

"What stamps!"

Kensal started to laugh at his own joke. Pinner didn't join him.

"There was a book, you know, The Collector. Same guy as wrote French Lieutenant's Woman."

"Yeah, right. See ya."

Frowning, Kensal watched Pinner turn to his cab.

"Good question for a crossword that," but Pinner was gone. Kensal's hand tightened slightly on the rolled newspaper.

Pinner was channel flicking: BBC 1, Thames, and back, when the phone rang. Pinner looked at it. He picked it up slowly as though sensing the unwelcome caller.

The man's voice was rough, a smoker's growl.

"Tony Pinner? Mr Pinner, my name is Detective Inspector Brough. I would appreciate it if you could spare me a few minutes…"

Pinner did not answer. Instead, he looked up from the phone towards Olympia, freshly bathed, who had just appeared in the doorway. Olympia could hear the man's voice on the phone.

"Mr Pinner? … Tony? … "

Olympia reached for the phone as Pinner set it back on its cradle.

"You're the good guy this time."

"Thought I was last time."

The phone rang again. They both started, looked at the phone, then at each other. This time Olympia reached the phone first.

Pinner hurried through the double doors of St. Thomas's hospital. Dodging a patient walking with two nurses, he glanced upward, scanning for a certain ward number: Ward 14, second floor.

He took the stairs two at a time, thrusting open the door to the second floor.

Pinner turned into the open ward and instantly spotted Beth sitting with Harold. Pinner's father looked grey. The rasp of his breath was short. Beth reached out for her son's hand.

Pinner was standing taking in fresh air with the smokers at the hospital entrance. Big, greedy, life-affirming breaths as his fear for his father rose.

"What do the doctors say?" The smoker's voice.

Pinner looked at the square, well-built man wrapped in a creased, slept-in raincoat. "Detective Inspector Brough."

Brough was older than Pinner, in his forties maybe. Tired with watchful eyes. Crumpled, almost scruffy except for the bright bow tie, that shouted out from the accompanying drab garb. Pinner pulled his eyes from the red and white splash of silk and found Brough's eyes. Small grey and steady.

The policeman offered Pinner a cigarette instead of a handshake. Pinner took it – Senior Service, his granddad's choice.

Brough lit his own, but Pinner looked at the fag in his hand in bemusement.

"I don't smoke."

Brough shrugged.

"Reflex action. Filthy habit."

Pinner returned the compliment.

"Coat needs a clean, too."

Brough laughed. They were on solid ground.

"Tell me about Crosse."

Pinner shrugged, then ran over it for the detective.

"Horse Guards, about 11am, last Tuesday, opposite the MoD. He was looking for a cab. I clocked him and some wanker cut me up. That's it."

Brough watched Pinner and flicked his ash.

"Describe him."

"Tall, thin, thinning, raincoat, brown leather case, satchel thing, seen better days."

Brough nodded.

"And the cab."

Pinner said nothing.

"Clock the number, Tony."

Pinner turned to face Brough and silently handed him back the unlit, unsmoked cigarette.

In the gloom of Ward 14, Beth was sitting with Harold, clasping his hand. Their son was standing by the window. Pinner looked down on London; a mosaic of street lights.

Pinner felt unsettled. He could trust Brough. He knew it at a glance, yet that only heightened his unease. In the past, Pinner's instinct had screamed at him like a siren to take a particular course. He'd fought it and messed up each time. This time, he'd listen. He'd never had a drag of a cigarette in his life, but he craved one now. Senior Service made him think of his granddad again and that strengthened his resolve. Inadvertently, or perhaps intentionally, the detective had created a bond.

Pinner turned and met his mother's eye. He made a decision and drew up the spare chair closer to the bed.

"Dad."

Harold turned and acknowledged his son.

"I'll live." A weak smile to carry the gag.

Pinner smiled, but Beth looked beyond it.

"Dad, who's The Collector?"

Harold's breathing changed, suddenly becoming more laboured. He tried to cover it, but both Beth and Pinner noticed it.

"I'll live." A croak this time.

Pinner looked down on his dad. All he could see was defiance and fear. He knew Harold would say no more.

Pinner drove his mum home. Beth was in the passenger section behind his seat. He kept looking at her, but she avoided his searching eyes in the mirror.

When the cab pulled up, Beth struggled out.

"Good night, son."

"See yer, mum."

Pinner watched her turn and walk away. He stared down the road ahead. He had felt certain his mum was struggling with something. A rap on the window pulled him back. Pinner started at the sound. He opened the window and Beth's proud face jutted in.

"He won't talk about it, but I will. You steer clear, Tone. They did for your granddad."

"Who?"

"Him. The Collector."

"Mum?"

"I don't know much. Best you speak to Moshie. Moshie Kent, he knows."

Beth was gone. Pinner looked exasperated and none the wiser; what the hell did Moshie Kent know?

In his hospital bed, Harold Pinner was lying looking out at the window. He looked frightened, his fingers curling to crumple his sheet into a fist.

CHAPTER 6

*T*HE TWO MEN WERE LIGHTING TORCHES. *They looked up and down the narrow lane. One stepped forward and lit a bundle of tinder propped against a building. The other moved across to light another. They worked their way down the street, setting it alight. The Street sign read 'Pudding Lane'.*

From a boat, the two men looked back at their handiwork as the flames from the fire spread through London's tight streets.

When Pinner woke, he could still smell the smoke. It clung to him as he dressed quickly. The dream had not been a good one and today was an early start.

Smithfield Market at dawn. Barrows of meat were being

hauled from the market into vans and trucks as Pinner's cab parked up.

There had been a meat market at Smithfield for centuries. Sir Horace Jones, the name came unbidden to Pinner, was the architect who had designed the market building. Like riding a bike, you never forgot details learnt as a Knowledge Boy.

Pinner watched two men struggle to hoist a huge carcass. Wat Tyler and William Wallace; two more names, but less comfortable ones. Both men had been butchered here, when Smithfield had served a darker purpose as the King's execution yard.

Moshie Kent had been a taxi driver. In fact, he was a celebrity cabbie. Punters loved him, his knowledge of the capital was legendary. But his delivery was the making of him. Regaling was an unused word these days, but that was Moshie for you. A smaller, more contained Henry Cooper.

He was an entertainer, a cabbie who could spin a yarn, from pick up to drop off. He was shrewd, too; he understood people and money. Diversification. That summed the man up, an investment here, a few pounds there. Soon he had a small business empire. Nothing flash, but Moshie soon found he didn't need to drive every day.

He'd been a family friend for years. Yet, somewhere lodged in Pinner's archive was a sense that his father, Harold, was uneasy in Moshie Kent's company. Jealousy? Yet Pinner had always got on well with the one-time boxer. He'd been one of Pinner's coaches at the Boys' Club, before Pinner had discovered music.

For a moment, Pinner could smell the sweat, taste the salt of blood in his mouth as he remembered the corner seat and the harsh, muscle-searing training regime. Pinner climbed out of his cab.

A market porter noticed Pinner's parked cab and started shaking his head.

"Hey, mate! You can't park there!"

Pinner considered the request.

"I'm here to see Mr Kent."

At that introduction, the porter checked and turned back to his work.

Pinner entered the market and walked down the avenue. It was a world of men in white coats and butchers' smocks. They were busy trading. The names of the companies painted above the stalls: Holt, Roberts, Essman. All the names were presented in the same font, the mark of the City of London Corporation.

Pinner had always liked markets: Smithfield, Billingsgate, Spitalfields, even Covent Garden. He loved the rough banter. Here everyone had a nickname and a reputation to defend, even for being useless. It counted for everything.

He especially liked markets before the buyers arrived, the smell, with the sense of impending rush.

Pinner stood watching a small, bow-legged man, giving instructions to two young lads.

"…and be sharp about it. No lagging."

Then Kent, in his sixties, but with good shoulders, shiny shoes and a boxer's face and gait, spied Pinner and his face lit up.

"Tony!"

They shook hands. Kent peered up at Pinner. His arrival had plainly made the older man's day.

"Come, you look in need of a feast. You've come to the right place."

Kent led Pinner a short distance to a polished wooden door, which he unlocked with an ancient key. They entered a small flat; passed a dated gas meter by the front door next to a rack of well-polished shoes, then up a small flight of stairs. Must help keep him fit, thought Pinner. He couldn't help noting the contrast with his own father's poor health. He pushed the thought away. Moshie had always been good to him. Pinner had been a favourite at the Repton Boys' Club.

"My small kingdom. Sit down, sit."

Pinner looked around the modest flat. It was like stepping inside the Tardis. Pinner thought of sitting watching Jon Pertwee, while Anthony hid behind the settee and it added to his sense of wellbeing. Being with Moshie did that for him, too.

He took a closer look at Moshie's room. The carpet had been expensive when it was laid, Axminster or something like that. There was a reading chair by the window, with a two-seater for guests. The sideboard doubled as a drinks cabinet.

Pinner sat at the small table. He looked around; a Coronation plate on one of the walls. Old, well-made furniture. It is a room out of time. Kent put a huge fry-up in front of him. He must have had it ready. The flat was warm from oven cooking.

"Beats café fare."

Kent laughed at his jibe. Pinner smiled, too, as Kent sat down and joined him, a plate of assorted meats in front of them.

"I heard about Harold. Give him my best. And your beautiful wife? Still got that tape somewhere," a pause then Kent hurried on, "women are, well, they have their own agenda, Tone. Marvellous and malevolent. Beautiful and ugly. How's the boy?"

"They're all well."

Kent's manners were good. There was something of James Mason in him, thought Pinner. The sausages were good, too.

"Must be six or so now."

"Who's The Collector?"

Kent's expression tightened involuntarily. Almost a shade, a reflex, of pain. He glanced at Pinner, then almost inadvertently over his shoulder. The older man took Pinner's arm and held it tight. The fork was halted in mid-air.

"That's not a question asked nor answered lightly. Have you been invited?"

Kent could see from Pinner's face this was not the case. Kent dabbed his month with his handkerchief.

"So you've crossed him."

"I don't even know who he is. I saw something, went to the police. No big deal. Except, I get this visit. Two blokes. Message from The Collector, warning me off."

Kent nodded cautiously as he chewed.

"Then this copper turns up. Wants more info."

"And?"

Pinner held Kent's gaze.

Kent pursed his lips and seemed even more uncertain as he studied Pinner's face. Kent pushed his plate, barely started, away from him. It was a small gesture, the moment before a storytelling starts.

"OK, for you," he paused, "The Collector is an office, an official. He collects from cabbies. Has done for years. Was a time, we saw him a lot."

"Protection?"

"More than that. Tone, leave it, son. Stall the copper. Tell him to sod off, damn him." Moshie had changed his mind. No story this time.

Pinner looked surprised at the language. So did Moshie, who was trying to collect himself.

"My pardon, it's just concern. I don't know who he is. Wouldn't recognise him if he dropped dead in front of me. But I know the stories. Just leave it."

Kent patted Pinner on the arm and picked up the plates. Pinner had had no more than a couple of mouthfuls of sausage.

"My love to your beautiful mother."

Pinner managed a smile, but still looked unconvinced. He realised Moshie Kent was scared and that he had been dismissed. In Moshie's eyes, Pinner was still the boy from the gym.

Kensal was chewing a pen, hunched over the racing form.

It was a habit he picked up as a teenager, after watching too many movies. Kensal loved films. If he was asked he'd always tell you: "Every film needs a really good baddie." It was all that mattered in a film to Kensal.

The door opened and Pinner sat down next to him. Toby did not look up. Today, his suit was mustard brown.

"How's tricks, mate?"

"Two teas please, Vicki."

Vicki smiled back at Pinner.

"OK. You?"

"Mustn't grumble."

"How's your day?"

Kensal looked up from his paper as Vicki placed two steaming mugs of tea in front of them. Ignoring his tea, Pinner got straight to the point.

"Your dad ever mention anything about The Collector, some sort…"

"You're not on that again!"

Pinner pressed on.

"I tried to speak to my dad. He got all flustered, but this Collector is real. He collects dues, he … people are scared of him. What he stands for."

Kensal looked bemused.

"Where did you get all this malarkey from?"

"I went to see Moshie Kent."

"That old tosser!"

It was then that both men realised Vicki was still standing there. Kensal scowled at the discovery.

"You can pay me later then."

Vicki smiled, but she had made her point. Both men

knew she heard the exchange. Pinner opened his wallet and Kensal spied the Ten Shilling note.

"Less than worthless, that is, mate," Kensal scoffed. He was right. Ten Shilling notes had ceased to be legal tender in November the previous year.

Pinner knew it, but like his cab, the small link to the past that the now defunct note gave him was a comfort; a reminder of better times. Pinner couldn't have said when… just a time when he had felt a better man.

"He told me The Collector has been around for years."

"What is he, blinking immortal?" Kensal scowled.

"The Collector must be his title. I think it might not be the same bloke."

"Like the bloody Lord Mayor."

Pinner was angry now and that was never a good thing. Kensal held up his hand. It was almost an apology.

"Alright. Suppose Moshie wasn't having you on. What's it got to do with you? Why the interest?"

"I got a visit from the police. Some Inspector. Wanted to talk about Crosse, you know the guy who went missing."

"Tell him to sod off," Kensal tapped his pen on the table to emphasise his point.

"After all, if this Collector character is some kind of gangster, you don't want to upset him, do you?"

Pinner nodded and Kensal, reassured, nodded back. Pinner stood and walked over to settle with Vicki at the counter.

"Thanks, Tony. Is he real?"

Pinner looked at her. Vicki met his gaze.

"I think so."

"Who's real?"

Olympia was standing in the kitchen. Pinner looked between the two women.

"I don't know."

Pinner's cab pulled out on to Kensington High Street. The FOR HIRE sign was on. A punter spotted him and signalled for the cab.

Pinner saw the fare, but kept driving.

It was something that he had only done once before, the night Anthony was born.

The punter made a rude gesture as Pinner ignored him and the cab flashed past. But giving the fingers to a missed cab never makes up for missing it.

Pinner was trawling his memory and he had a good one. As a boy, Pinner had spent a lot of time with his granddad, Harold. King Harold, Pinner had crowned him secretly as a boy. Like Pinner, Harold had a fighter's broad shoulders and imposing chest. He was a man to be reckoned with. But mainly, Pinner remembered his laugh. It came from deep down and wrapped people up. He had that knack, that gift, of making people feel better simply for knowing him. Even for passing him in the street.

Pinner also remembered when he died; a hit and run. Scores of cabbies had joined the police in trying to find the driver, but he was never traced. His parents never spoke of it. Until, his mum's words: "They did for your grandfather."

Pinner drove on through Knightsbridge, passing

three women carrying a homemade sign '8% sorry wrong number'; postal workers heading back from a rally. Pinner was glad he had missed it.

Further east, approaching Goodge Street, Angel was driving, with Morden in the back counting envelopes. Morden looked up from his calculations.

"This will do."

Angel nodded in the mirror and pulled the cab over next to an empty telephone box.

Morden climbed out nimbly and disappeared inside the faded red box. He dialled quickly. The phone was answered on the first ring.

"About time." muttered Morden.

He cut short the conversation: "It's genuine. The price is not negotiable. Right. We'll meet him then."

Vicki was testing Preston in a corner of the café when Pinner came in. Vicki looked up and moved her eyes towards a man sitting in the corner, nursing a steaming mug of tea. The man was Detective Inspector Brough, sporting a blue and yellow silk bow tie today. To Pinner's eye, it looked like the only item of clothing he had changed.

Pinner stood before his table as Brough looked up.

"Nothing new with you, Anthony?"

Pinner shook his head, turned and walked out, leaving

Vicki looking concerned. Preston had also followed the exchange. They shared a worried glance. Not so, Brough, who took another sip of his mug and offered them a resigned smile, as though people ran away from him every day.

A vehicle pulled up in the gloom of Gawber Street. The door opened and footsteps approached Pinner's cab.

Leather gloved hands flicked open a slim switchblade.

It made a faint glint under the streetlight.

CHAPTER 7

SQUINTING AGAINST THE RISING SUN, PINNER turned and locked his front door, tugging on his leather jacket, but Pinner's steps faltered as he approached his cab. He stood and shook his head in disbelief.

His cab was slumped on four flat tyres.

Pinner was standing waiting at Kipping's Yard, as Eddie the mechanic emerged from the gloom.

Eddie called him over.

"Tone. You better take a look at this."

Pinner followed Eddie into the garage, which was set into a cavernous railway arch.

In the centre of the workshop, Pinner's cab was up on jacks. Eddie crouched and Pinner followed his example.

"They're all the same. Small puncture. A very sharp blade. I'd say you've got a fan club, Tone."

Pinner chewed on this.

The heavy curtains had been pulled around the bed that Harold Pinner was lying in. He peered up into the curtains' shadows. He was not alone, standing in the corner was the outline of a man.

"Remember those two old knights, Discretion and Valour."

Harold followed the words with his fixed, frightened eyes.

"We know we can rely on you, Harold."

Pinner tried to open his front door, only to find it was locked. He looked up and down the street. The door opened fractionally, but the chain was on. Olympia's dark eyes stared out at him. Scared eyes. She unhooked the chain and stepped back to let him in.

"What's with the chain?"

"Hurry."

Pinner considered his options and stepped inside, both puzzled and annoyed. Olympia slammed the door behind him and hurriedly put the chain on again.

Pinner followed Olympia down the hall into the lounge.

Olympia paced around the room, her shoulders bunched in fear and anger.

"They were here. Here. Our home. Anthony's home. I told them that. What are you mixed up in?"

"Who were here?"

"Two of them. One small guy and a tall one. White guys."

Olympia waited. Pinner said nothing. She flicked her hair back, something she did when either angry or scared. Right now, she was scared.

"What did they want?"

Olympia put her hands to her face. Pinner moved towards her, but she motioned for him to stop.

"Said you'd made a mistake, but that you'd rectify it. See the error of your ways."

"Where's Ant?"

"Anthony is next door with Alice. What have you done, Tony?"

"I wish I knew."

Olympia was confused, her anger and fear growing. Both rising.

"These guys, they... they scared me. They scared Anthony."

"Maybe you should stay at Alice's tonight."

"Answer me!"

"I haven't got one, Pia."

Pinner looked anxious. Some unpleasant pieces were beginning to fall into place.

A cab pulled up outside Beth's house. Angel's face in the side mirror was scanning the road.

Satisfied, Angel turned off the ignition and turned back towards Morden, perched on the passenger seats.

"No sign."

Morden lit a cigarette, enjoying the moment.

"We'll wait."

Angel put the radio on and 'Love Grows Where My Rosemary Goes' enveloped them. Morden frowned at him, but said nothing, merely flicked his ash out of the cab window. He drummed his fingers on the window while waiting.

Morden's fingers were tapping out a rhythm to 'I Hear You Knocking'. Suddenly, he snapped his fingers. Angel switched the radio volume the wrong way. Dave Edmonds's voice filled the cab, buffeting them, causing Morden to scowl and Angel hastily switched the radio off. Angel followed Morden's line of sight to where Beth Pinner was labouring with a small over-full shopping bag. They watched her progress towards them.

Beth Pinner turned into her small strip of garden. She fished out her key, but as she did so, Beth stopped and turned to face the road. She stared straight at the cab. The two men stared back, slightly caught out, but defiant.

Beth straightened her back and opened her front door. She disappeared inside, leaving the door wide open.

Morden and Angel watched her. They waited for the open door to close, but Beth did not return.

Morden considered his nails, then made a decision and climbed out of the back of the cab.

Morden and Angel cautiously approached the front door, both looking uncertain. As they reached the door, they looked at each other, trying to fathom what to do next.

"Come in! Leave the door open."

Morden nodded slowly, a small smile rising. Angel, however, looked confused. This was bizarre.

They entered the house, moving cautiously down the hall, and turned into the lounge.

Beth was sitting in Harold's chair, tea and scones on a small table.

"Milk?"

Morden smiled. He appreciated bravado. He took a seat on the sofa indicated by Beth, while Angel remained standing, the more uneasy of the two. Beth served them both tea with ceremony.

"Come to give me a duffing up or do you have something else in mind?"

Morden's smile was approving.

"You've got balls, Mrs Pinner."

"You left school too early, son."

"Nice tea. Earl Gray?"

"Darjeeling, the champagne of teas. I don't hold with tea bags."

"When's he back?"

"Doctors wouldn't say."

"Tony?"

Beth passed Morden a scone, but he declined.

"He works irregular hours."

Morden, teacup and saucer in his hands, leaned forward, his tone confiding.

"His mother, his wife, his mates. No one seems to know his habits. Perhaps we should ask someone else. His father, not in good health, I hear. Sorry to hear it. His son?"

For the first time, Beth looked uncertain.

"Nice lad. Doing well at school, is he?"

The cup in Beth's hand started shaking, the tea spilling over into the saucer. Fear or anger, Morden did not care. He just needed Pinner. Morden leaned in and lifted the teacup gently out of her hands. He smiled at Beth.

"Oldman's Garage, six o'clock. Tell him."

Slowly, he laid Beth's cup and saucer down, respectful of the delicate china.

Morden paused at the door.

"Sons should listen to their mothers."

Pinner's cab swung into the deserted forecourt of Oldman's Garage. The garage was abandoned, near derelict, and had been since the owner had keeled over with a heart attack eight years ago. His son ran a night club and had no interest in the site. Pinner knew the boy, by reputation anyway, as a vicious bully.

The engine was killed as Pinner sat in the shadowed cab. He was tense and watchful.

Pinner waited, a tension growing in his shoulders and neck. His mum's call had caused panic initially, but now a slow rage was building in his chest. My family. My son.

A second cab pulled in, its lights dipping as it turned off the road. Pinner watched it come to a halt. He heard the handbrake being applied. Slowly, almost feeling his way in the dark, Pinner climbed out of the cab.

The trio stood facing each other. Pinner, with his cab at his back. Angel and Morden a few yards away. *My enemy*.

"You disappoint me, Tony. A simple request to show some restraint. You chose to ignore it."

Pinner was silent.

"You know this policeman, this Brough?"

"I've only met him twice."

"Once was enough. I thought we agreed."

"Maybe you should tell him that."

Morden studied Pinner, who stepped forward as if accepting the challenge.

"Why the heavy handedness? Visiting my family – putting the frighteners on them?"

"We're done."

Morden held up a finger.

"One more strike and you're out."

Morden turned away, but Pinner was not finished.

"So, that's it. Tony be a good boy or what?"

As Pinner stepped towards the departing Morden, Angel stepped in and slammed his fist into Pinner's midriff. Pinner collapsed. Morden paused at the cab door and looked back.

"A taster, Tony. My apprentice is quite adept."

Pinner was on his knees gasping for breath as Angel eased the steel knuckleduster off his fist. Morden closed the door of the cab and walked back towards Pinner. The kick was short and sharp. Pinner went down, his face hitting the tarmac. The cab's engine was gunned, as Pinner tried to clear the ringing in his head.

Angel's cab moved off as Pinner struggled to haul himself up. Pinner stared at the cab. He could just make out that Angel was driving and in the back, next to Morden, Pinner could see the outline of another shadowy figure.

Pinner was left, wounded, hurt and defiant.

CHAPTER 8

K ENSAL WAS IN HIS USUAL SEAT AT Olympia's, his face deep in the sports' pages.

"Another defeat. How many is that? So much for getting it out of their system." Kensal spoke as if it was the Original Sin he was talking about.

West Ham's season had been a poor one thus far, with a string of disappointing results since before Christmas.

"It all started with that cup debacle up in Blackpool.

"Mind you, losing a few football games is one thing, but at least they didn't get beaten up," finished Kensal.

He looked up. Pinner was sitting slumped against the wall. Pinner's face was grazed and the bruises were already darkening.

"Who were they? Turks?"

There had been talk of the Turkish gangs making a bid for a slice of the protection rackets in London over the past year. Trying to fill the void after some of the capital's leading villains had been jailed.

Pinner shook his head, although it still hurt to do so.

"No, no. They were… like us. You and me, Londoners."

Kensal looked dismissive, but Pinner made his point.

"Cabbies."

"Cabbies. Like us."

Kensal cast an annoyed glance at the young Scot sitting with them.

"Like us? You're not a cabbie or a Londoner. Get us a coffee and a tea."

Preston looked about to protest, but Kensal stared him down. Reluctantly, Preston arrived at the counter.

"Men's talk."

Vicki looked unimpressed, but cast a concerned eye towards Pinner.

"He got a hiding," explained Preston quietly.

"I'll bring them over."

Preston and Vicki exchanged conspirators' smiles.

Kensal frowned as Preston slumped down next to him again.

"Just drop it, mate. You've been down on your luck. You saw something, now you're being asked to unsee it."

Preston shook his head.

"Something happened to this guy, this Civil Servant boy."

Vicki chipped in.

"Something bad."

Kensal was irritated.

"Bad? He's dead isn't he?"

Vicki put the mugs down.

"And the same could happen to you."

Preston and Vicki looked at Kensal with contempt. Kensal held his hands up.

"Alright, I'm no hero. But I know that. But it's not just you I'm thinking of."

Pinner cast his friend a dark glance.

Preston was looking at Kensal, but Vicki was studying Pinner's bruised profile. He was staring outside. She followed his gaze, to find it was fixed on a squat black cab parked across the road.

Pinner turned back to the others.

Kensal repeated his question.

"I said, where's Olympia today?"

Brough emerged from the Paddington Police Station and walked across to the newspaper cabin leaning against the nearby corner shop. A black cab trailed him slowly. Unnoticed by him, Brough was being watched through the passenger window mirror.

Brough paid for a paper and some cigarettes. As he turned away, the black cab swung round, so that as Brough looked to cross the road he was cut off. Annoyed, he crouched forward to look across at the driver.

"Get in."

Brough folded his paper and climbed into the back. As Pinner drove off, Brough settled back, resisting the urge to light a cigarette. Pinner's voice was low. So low that Brough had to lean forward to catch it all.

Half an hour later, Pinner's cab was parked on a dingy section of wasteland overlooking the Thames, east of Tower Bridge. Pinner was leaning against the bonnet of his cab. Brough stood, his back to Pinner, studying the river and smoking.

"Some tale, Tony."

Brough turned back towards him.

"Make a good book. The Collector."

"It was a book. So my mate says."

"I've been in the Met for 20 years and I've heard some tales, but this is a tall one. All right, OK, I'll look into it. It's Crosse that interests me."

"What did he do?"

"He was bloody murdered."

"No. I meant…"

"Oh. The Treasury. A Think Tank boffin."

Brough looked out across the Thames.

"We fished him out not far from here." Pinner followed Brough's gaze out at the dark Thames water.

"Any chance of a lift?" asked Brough, before he crushed his cigarette under his shoe.

Across from Paddington Police Station, Brough climbed out of Pinner's cab. He raised his paper at Pinner as he drove off. Unseen by Brough and Pinner, sitting across at the front of a taxi rank was a cab, its TAXI sign on; the number plate read SE1 4PE.

Pinner turned into Gawber Street. He slowed, with his house still 30 yards away, eyes scanning ahead. A single cab was parked outside his house. Pinner drew up to the curve of the street, giving him the better vantage point. He had almost expected this.

He looked up and down the street, but he could not make out the number plate of the waiting cab, but he didn't really need to – he knew. The light was on in his house. He flicked the indicator switch and executed a seamless arc in the narrow street, swinging the cab in the opposite direction.

His mum's was out of bounds, too, he realised. Pinner studied his watch, not too late, he figured. Without conscious effort, his mind mapped out the route to Preston and Vicki's small flat. Eighteen minutes at this time of night.

Less than 17 minutes later, Pinner's cab pulled up outside Preston and Vicki's flat.

Vicki was sitting on the settee, coffee in hand, with a biscuit for dunking in the other, laughing at a TV sitcom, 'The Lovers'. Vicki had a thing about Richard Beckinsale.

The doorbell rang and Vicki jolted up, looked at her watch. She went to the curtains and took in the distinctive outline of Pinner's cab.

Vicki hurried to the door. She took off the chain and opened it. Pinner shrugged by way of apology.

"Sorry."

"No. Come in."

Preston appeared behind her.

"Welcome to Preston's Palace," grinned the effervescent young Scot.

"He's the chef tonight." Vicki smiled at her man.

Perched on a large sofa in Vicki's compact lounge, Pinner was on the phone. The room had the feel of a domesticated student flat; tidy, but not pristine.

"Is Alice OK with that? Right, you stay there. Yeah. Bye, Pia."

Pinner looked up to find Vicki and Preston watching him from the doorway.

Pinner was sitting on the settee, as he scanned a phone directory. Preston passed him a glass of whisky.

"I'm driving."

"Got somewhere else in mind."

Pinner frowned, then smiled. Preston returned it.

"Uncle Preston's here to help."

Pinner studied the young Scot as Preston raised his glass to him. Pinner nodded and tasted the liquor.

CHAPTER 9

A MAN WAS BEING BUNDLED OUT OF A CAB, *dragged by two others. He was struggling, but the other two knew what they were doing. The driver watched as they stabbed him. The victim slumped against the wall, as his assailants climbed back into the cab.*

Pinner woke up on the settee. Sunlight poured through the blinds as Pinner awoke. He sat up, sweat coated him as though he had been in the struggle.

The directory was still on the coffee table. He pulled on his shoes and picked up a piece of paper. The directory page was open at CROSSE.

In the bedroom, Vicki was asleep. She stirred at the careful closing of a door. The noise woke her and she struggled up. From outside, the dull thud of a car door closing reached her. She watched from her window as Pinner drove off.

Preston sat up in bed.

"What's going on, Preston?

"We'll see him later."

Pinner's heavy finger pressed the doorbell of a suburban post-war semi-detached London villa. It chimed weakly. Pinner pressed it again. No reply. An old, but well-cared for, Rover was parked in the driveway.

Pinner edged past it and walked around the back of the house. He reached the back gate and leaned over to lift the latch.

"Stop there! I've had enough of you press people."

Pinner peered over the gate. Mrs Crosse, a slim, colourless woman was staring at him.

"Go away. I'm calling the police."

"Please, Mrs Crosse. I'm a cabbie. I know your husband. My name's Tony Pinner. I saw him last week."

Mrs Crosse's fingers tighten on her skirt, but she nodded slowly.

"The taxi man."

Mrs Crosse led the way into her house. Pinner followed, taking in the immaculately groomed garden.

Pinner sat awkwardly on a chair in the Crosse's living room. Mrs Crosse did not seem to know whether to sit or stand. The lounge was flowery, as if the house would rather have been in the country. Perhaps Mrs Crosse would have, too. She looked as if the garden and the local Pony Club would suit her more than being a suburban widow.

"Drink? Would you…" She started to move.

"Tea would be lovely, thanks, please."

"I meant a drink."

Mrs Crosse was at the drinks' cabinet. She poured herself one. Pinner watched her, then the wall-clock, which read just after 10am.

"Just a small one, then."

Mrs Crosse handed him his drink and took a sip of hers, before she sat down across from him.

"Makes a change speaking to someone else. Not police or reporter types."

Pinner nodded, but did not take a sip of his drink. He needed his wits.

"How did he look that morning?"

Pinner looked uncertain how to proceed now that he was perched in Crosse's home; in the living room of a dead man. However, Mrs Crosse, after her initial hostility, seemed almost grateful for his visit.

"In the pink, I suppose. He hailed me, but someone else picked him up. Another cab."

"It's a cut-throat business, I guess."

She took another swallow.

"Thursday was his big day. Used to call it the Chancellor's Tea Party."

Pinner looked at a loss, so Mrs Cross helped him out.

"His day with the boss.

"His real boss. Not the Chancellor of the Exchequer, the Prime Minister. I think he's a distant man, but Howard said he had vision. Balliol men together.

"A man not afraid to leap in the dark. That's what he

said. When I saw your cab, I thought it might be him and we could just forget that he's gone. Do you think we could do that?"

Pinner's cab was parked outside Highbury football ground. The Arsenal had a strong team at present, but weekdays it was quiet. Pinner's beloved West Ham had a strong squad, too, but he was close to losing faith with the side's tired stars. Bonds and Lampard had heart, and he admired young Best, but his hopes for the future were pinned on Brooking. Perhaps it was a team of false promises, but he'd always be an Iron.

He had stopped going for a while when Olympia and the band had been getting the better gigs like Ronnie Scott's, but they had not cracked The Big Time and neither had the Hammers.

In the shadow of his team's arch rivals, Pinner was sitting in the back of his cab, surrounded by papers and magazines: The Economist, The Financial Times, business pages of other publications. He was scanning all the articles.

Preston was sitting reading a magazine when Pinner entered Olympia's. On the radio, Clive Dunn was droning on about 'Granddad'.

"You should be studying."

Preston was pleased to see him despite the jibe. Vicki looked up from the hotplate and also smiled at Pinner.

"Seen Toby?"

Preston shook his head. Vicki arrived bearing a mug of tea and a bacon roll.

"On the house."

Pinner shared her smile, as Preston indicated a chair. Hesitantly, Pinner sat down. They both studied him.

"Back in a min."

Vicki headed to serve another customer.

Pinner looked up from his butty.

"You follow the stock market, Preston?"

"I canna afford my bus fare. But, yeah, a bit."

Pinner took another bite of his roll and stopped. The door swung open and Pinner looked to the door. Vicki swung round, sensing the change in atmosphere in the café.

"Morning, Tony. Old habits die hard, I see."

Pinner looked up at Morden and Angel. Other customers, cabbies mainly, eyed the two new arrivals with suspicion and disquiet.

"Spare us a few minutes."

Morden indicated they should leave.

"You can say it here."

Morden studied Pinner and surveyed the room. Everyone but Vicki and Preston averted their gazes.

"You must get it from your mum."

"Leave my mum out of this," Pinner stood up.

"Got a cab waiting for you, Tony."

Preston stood, too.

Morden considered him, but Preston stared back defiantly. Morden looked back to Pinner. Pinner shook his head at Preston, but the young Scot did not back off.

"You're not going anywhere, Tony."

In a single movement, Morden head-butted Preston, who rocked backwards, blood bursting from his wrecked nose. Morden stepped in to send the young Scot face down on to the table.

Pinner held up his hands. He nodded at Morden then slowly leaned in to examine Preston's smashed nose. Preston stared at him through one bloodied eye. Unseen by Morden and Angel, Pinner slipped his keys into Preston's pocket with one hand, while he looked at Preston's smashed nose. Preston, still dazed, tried to nod, but Pinner's tightened grip cautioned him.

Pinner straightened up and threw his mug of tea at Morden and rushed him, but he was outnumbered and outclassed. Together, Morden and Angel, subdued Pinner in seconds, with a few sharp body blows using a small kosh that appeared almost magically in Angel's hand. They manhandled him out of the café, spilling tables and chairs as they went. Vicki was yelling at them to stop. The other diners had all backed up against the walls, away from the upturned chairs and tables. One man stepped forward gingerly, but Angel pointed his kosh in the man's face and he remained still.

Vicki watched as Pinner was dragged out of the café and roughly bundled into a cab.

Vicki looked across at the other men, a couple pulled their coats on to leave, almost to cover their shame. A few slowly started eating again. Preston was now sitting upright, blood running down his face as Angel's cab drove off. In Preston's hands were the keys to Pinner's cab.

Tony Pinner was pressed in the back with Morden. He looked across at him, contempt and fear on his face. Morden merely smiled and patted Pinner's hand, a gentle menacing gesture.

Angel's cab crawled slowly along Southend's sombre, out of season, seaside frontage. The cab stopped in front of an ageing fun palace and Morden guided Pinner out. Pinner turned to follow the flight of a lone seagull high above them.

He was led into the funhouse; past ancient slot machines, a painted clown in a glass case. They reached the back of the building, the home to a small faded bingo hall.

There, Pinner was roughly plonked onto a small, round stool. Morden sat down next to him, as Pinner got his bearings.

Angel lowered himself onto the stool at the other side of Pinner. To steady himself, Pinner looked around the faded relic of an arcade. It was gloomy, with light coming from only the raised bingo caller's chair. The sphere containing the multi-coloured bingo balls suddenly lit up and the brightly coloured balls began to jump around.

Against this movement, the bingo caller's voice was both muffled and magnified.

"Eyes down then, your first number. On the blue four and eight, 48."

Pinner looked up at the bingo caller's chair, but he could not see who was there; the light sprayed straight into his eyes, leaving him squinting. He tried to shade his face.

To add to his disorientation, the bingo caller's voice was distorted by the microphone.

"Been here before, Tony?"

"As a kid."

"Seems you haven't grown up."

"Why are we here?"

Pinner looked around, taking in his surroundings, but he was struggling to focus.

"You've been a bad boy, Tony. Mingling with people you shouldn't."

Pinner seemed miles away. He focused on the bingo caller, trying to make him out, but it was futile.

"What did this copper, this Brough, what did he want?"

"Just Crosse."

The unseen man considered this and Pinner. Morden was studying his nails. He looked up and smiled at Pinner. Pinner sat upright, with the cold realisation that he was on trial.

"How's Mrs Crosse?"

Pinner watched another ball come out of the bubble.

"On the white six and one, 61. A good year."

Pinner and Morden looked at each other. Morden patted Pinner's knee.

"House."

Morden's voice was an affectionate whisper.

The sun was dropping on the beach, silhouetting the pier.

Pinner was standing at the end of the pier. Morden, wrapped in black coat, stood a few feet in front of him. Angel was at Pinner's back.

Pinner stared straight at Morden.

"What's so important about Crosse? What happened to him?"

At a signal from Morden, Angel snapped a fist into Pinner's kidneys. Pinner doubled, but stayed on his feet, the old boxing instincts kicking in.

Morden's blow was a blurred arc, that bent Pinner low.

Morden's voice was a whisper.

"It was a polite request."

As Pinner straightened, he got more of the same. This time, he was sent to his knees.

The kick was short and vicious.

Pinner was hauled up from his knees. Morden was close, the smell of mints and aftershave. Morden smiled at him.

"Tony, you should have thought of others; your father and your boy."

Pinner looked up at the switchblade in Morden's gloved hand. The image of his father and his son flashed through Pinner's mind.

"Taxi for Pinner."

Exploding, Pinner charged at Morden.

"No!"

Pinner crashed into Morden, sweeping the smaller man into the railings at the end of the pier.

Pinner smashed his forearm into Morden's face. Angel was two steps behind, reaching out to grab Pinner.

In a fluid motion, Pinner stepped onto the railing, looking back at the fallen Morden and the lunging Angel.

Morden's face was twisted, mouth open in rage.

"NO!"

Pinner leapt from the pier towards the black sea.

Morden and Angel peered over the railings at the dark water below.

"Shit."

The icy impact of the sea knocked some of the air out of Pinner's lungs, but he had enough left to swim on, further out beneath the surface.

Pinner emerged from the sea, weighed down by his sea-sodden clothes. The pier was some distance along the beach, like the broken silhouette of a Victorian dinosaur.

Angel and Morden's taxi was parked outside Southend railway station. Angel was at the wheel, engine purring, while Morden had tucked himself into a shadowed doorway, watching. Both were on the look out for Pinner.

In a quiet street not far from the seafront, Pinner stood in the still evening next to a parked car, a small hook of wire in his hand. He studied the car he had chosen. Nothing too flash, nothing too new, nothing worth noticing.

Pinner was driving. The road sign ahead read Central London 6 Miles. He made a point of carefully watching his speed. He only needed to reach the capital's outskirts.

Pinner walked towards Elm Park Tube Station, having left the stolen car parked carefully two streets away.

Pinner fed coins into the slot inside a dilapidated telephone box. He just hoped he could remember the number.

In the safety of Preston and Vicki's small flat, Pinner struggled to take off his sea-stained jacket. Olympia was on the phone.

"OK, thanks, Alice."

Olympia saw Pinner was struggling and moved to help him.

As she removed his T-shirt, she saw that Pinner's ribs were darkly bruised.

They looked at each other for a moment before Vicki appeared in the doorway, she, too took in the welts on Pinner's torso.

"I'll run a bath."

Vicki headed to the bathroom.

"I'll get rid of the cab."

Pinner shook his head at Preston's suggestion.

"I'll do it."

Preston looked at Pinner's battered state. Olympia, taking charge, nodded to Preston and threw him the keys to Pinner's pride and joy.

"Park her up somewhere safe," but Preston had already gone.

In a small City bar, Morden was sitting talking to another two men. The conversation was becoming agitated. Morden leaned in closer and the two men moved back in their seats. It was done subconsciously, but with real reason. Reluctantly, one nodded to the other as he handed over an envelope.

Morden accepted it and rose from the table. Both men watched him leave. One silently mouthed the word 'Tosser' to Morden's slim, tailored back.

Morden emerged from the pub, where Angel was standing with the two doormen. They were appeared deferential to Angel and Morden. Their reputation was growing.

As Morden and Angel climbed into the cab, the radio cracked into life.

"Caller to SE1 6NG. Joe sighted Arundal Grove, off Woodville. Pick up and despatch."

Angel picked up the radio. He looked back at Morden, who was counting money in the back seat. Morden nodded.

"Received SE1 6NG."

Angel flicked off the radio.

In the narrow street known as Arundal Grove, Angel's cab slowed up. Parked less than 20 yards away was Pinner's majestic old cab. Slowly Angel drew up behind it.

Pinner was sitting on Vicki's sofa, hair still wet, when Olympia carried in a tray.

"Cocoa."

Pinner did not respond.

"Tony."

Olympia sat on the sofa arm.

"They'll find me."

Olympia reached out and touched his shoulder.

"Not if you find them first."

Pinner gave Olympia a long stare, weighing the choice and the challenge she had given him.

Camera flashes bounced off the cold starkness of Heathrow's Terminal 1.

At the Airport Arrivals, the delegation of European financiers was standing, surrounded by a corps of press photographers. The three men, all in serious expensive suits, were hemmed in. They posed for a picture, but waved aside questions, as police officers gradually edged the ruck of journalists and a television crew backwards towards the waiting sleek line of Jaguars.

On the right, stood Herr Freimann, a distinguished looking man in his fifties. He smiled for the cameras, the kind dispensed by dentists to their patients in the chair as it reclined. His thoughts were elsewhere. He looked beyond the press pack.

Standing 20 feet away, were Morden and Angel.

Brough's office was a cramped ill-lit cupboard. Even the powerful desk lamp failed to dispel the feeling that the dark corners of the confined space were edging towards the desk.

The Inspector was flicking through a file. Howard Crosse's file: a picture of Crosse, a statement from his wife, a picture of Crosse with the Prime Minister, another from his university days.

The door opened a fraction and a hard-faced sergeant leaned in.

"You'll want to see this, sir."

A black cab was slowly pulled out of the Thames. The crane doing the work was perched on a square of wasteland, between two modern blocks of flats with intercom security. Brough understood people's fears; across the river was Rotherhithe.

The new apartments had small two-seater balconies. Just room enough for a couple and their gin and tonics, he thought. Swinging a cat wasn't an option, but you could hang one out there.

Water showered down from the vehicle's windows and side doors.

The cascading water brought Brough's mind back to

the job in hand. The cab was a dead weight at the end of the giblet. Perhaps that was where the thought had come from.

Brough and his sergeant, a brute of a man called Collier, stood watching as the cab was swung to the ground. The crane driver carefully manoeuvred the wreckage on to its wheels before he gave the waiting officers the thumbs up.

Police divers were clambering out of the water. Encased in black, moving slowly on the rough ground, one of them spied Brough and walked across to meet him. Brough and his sergeant walked across to the cab.

The diver turned to them.

"Sir."

Brough recognised him as he tugged off his goggles.

"Ted."

"Male. White. About five ten, I reckon."

Brough's gloved hand pulled the driver's door open.

"Pinner…"

Water poured out as the door swung open. The pale hair-matted face of Preston poured out with it.

Brough took a step back.

"That him, sir?"

"That's his cab. Get an ID on him."

Brough turned away lighting a cigarette. He was troubled, a growing sickness in his stomach that only nicotine would sedate.

CHAPTER 10

*T*HE WELL-DRESSED GENTLEMAN CLIMBED *into the back of a cab, sporting an elegant grey suit with a flower in the button hole. He pulled out a silver cigarette case, engraved with a coat of arms and the motto 'Ich Dien'.*

Olympia shook Pinner awake. He looked up blurry-eyed. The dream had lacked the enveloping sense of menace of his recent visions, but it had still left him with a feeling of unease; a sense of loss. She smiled uncertainly.

"Coffee's on."

Pinner swung himself up. *'Ich Dien', I serve.*

Olympia put the coffee in front of him. Pinner noticed her legs and her state of dress. She just had a sleeping T-shirt on.

Olympia perched on the edge of the sofa bed, but there was still a distance between them. Pinner was conscious of that.

"Tony."

"I don't know."

"Go to the police."

"He doesn't believe me."

"We'll all go. Me, Preston and Vicki."

Pinner shook his head.

"I've got things to do first."

Olympia looked bewildered. Pinner pulled on his crumpled shirt. *I serve.*

Angel's cab pulled up at the entrance to the Dorchester Hotel, on Park Lane. The doorman came across and leaned in, indicating that the cab should move on, but Angel ignored him, fingering the worn knuckleduster in his suit pocket.

Herr Freimann walked down the steps from the hotel and to the cab. The doorman hastily adjusted his stance and opened the cab door for the distinguished looking guest.

Freimann met Angel's eyes in the mirror with a cool calm and nodded.

Pinner came around the corner heading towards Preston's flat, carrying a bottle of milk and a newspaper. He suddenly checked, taking in the police officer stationed outside Preston's flat. Hastily, he stepped back. Hoping he had avoided notice.

Then he realised there were more police officers along the road. He edged back, taking a long, slow breath to release the panic that would have caused him to bolt. He remained unseen, but shaken.

As Pinner watched, Vicki was led out. She was crying and was being helped along by an officer. DI Brough emerged at the entrance to the flat. He was giving instructions to junior officers.

Vicki was escorted into one of the waiting police cars. Brough was standing, ritually lighting a cigarette as Vicki was driven off in a car.

Pinner watched her pale face in the rear window as the vehicle swept past.

Pinner turned his attention back to the detective. The expression on Brough's face was bleak. It matched Pinner's.

Pinner was waiting in Kipping's Yard. Eddie emerged from the gloom and handed over the keys to him. Pinner looked at the black cab, a nondescript modern model compared to Pinner's own.

"She's better than she looks," confided Eddie, a gentle sales pitch.

"Thanks, Eddie. I owe you one," Pinner said, as he climbed into the cab. From the window, he turned to Eddie.

"And remember, Eddie."

"Yeah, yeah."

Eddie waved Pinner's words aside, but Pinner was

looking elsewhere, focusing on a cab lifted on hydraulic jacks in the garage, a mechanic examining its under carriage. Its number plate read SE11 6NP. Giving nothing away, Pinner gave Eddie a wave and drove off. Pinner looked back in his mirror to see Eddie waving him off. Only then did he allow himself a slight frown. He was beginning to notice small details.

Pinner's new cab was parked up outside an old lock up. The ancient wooden doors were crying out for paint; the wood at the floor was damp and split. Pinner was working the lock. It was stubborn with age and rust, but yielded eventually.

Olympia helped him push the doors open.

"My dad's old lock-up. Forgot I still had a key."

Olympia nodded slowly. Revisiting old haunts made her uneasy; shades of happier times.

"You took me here before. Years ago."

They looked at each other, both remembering.

"It was freezing then, too."

Pinner smiled slightly, but Olympia would not meet his eye.

The door finally opened fully with a final shove.

Pinner switched on the light, revealing a disused garage; an old blanket covered a sofa, crates and an assortment of taxi accessories from old models. Sitting silently was the outline of an Austin FX3. It had been kept for parts. One man's small shrine. Harold's temple.

Pinner was already looking for something, while Olympia was concentrating on trying to stay warm. Her impatience helped, she wanted answers.

"Tony."

Pinner straightened.

"Need to find dad's old plates," but Olympia still looked confused and concerned.

"They're looking for me."

Pinner put his hands on her arms and rubbed them to put in warmth and to get the message across.

"I think they found Preston," his voice quiet.

Olympia looked from Pinner's face to the bunch of keys in his hands. Olympia opened her mouth as she took in what Pinner was implying. No sound came.

Pinner drew her to him and held her as his eyes roamed the room searching for the plates.

Beth Pinner was closing up the launderette. Squashed on the corner of Bethnal Green Road and Potts Road, it was a steady little earner; not that Beth spent the money, she was saving for Anthony. The little boy was her focus and her future.

As she turned the final key and dropped the heavy mortice latch, a figure stepped towards her from under a nearby streetlight. Beth turned to face him, gathering herself and her courage.

"You gave me a fright."

Brough stepped out completely of the gloom.

"I need to find him, Mrs Pinner."

"You think he did it?"

"He came to me."

"Yes. Yes, he did and you didn't believe him."

"How's your husband?"

Brough lit a cigarette.

"Dying."

Brough took in the smoke with a sharper drag. The barb had stuck.

"We're done here. I've got a husband to visit."

Beth pushed past the policeman, her head held high. The detective let her pass. Unseen by him, she had tears in her eyes, but her stride was strong.

Olympia, her face tear-stained, hauled open the Lock-up doors. As she drew them wide, Pinner was behind the wheel of his new taxi cab and slowly edged the cab into the lock up. Olympia closed the double doors behind him.

As Pinner climbed out of the cab, Olympia passed him a small rectangular canvas package. Pinner pulled it open to reveal an old set of taxi plates. They were old, thought Pinner, wouldn't pass a close inspection either, but it was the best he had and going back to see Eddie was out of the question.

They looked at each other for a moment. Olympia nodded – a show of shared strength.

The pair began to change the plates together.

It was progress, he supposed. They haven't even helped

each other change a light bulb for months now, thought Pinner, as he took the first plate from his wife. Admiring her long, smooth fingers as he did so.

Brough, carrying coffee in an enamel mug, walked towards his office. The canteen brew was almost unbearable, but this far into an investigation, it was a necessary sufferance.

As a shapely young officer walked past him, she raised her eyebrows at him. Brough frowned. He was not the kind of man that women, even in uniform, flirted with.

His frown grew as he entered his office and found a senior uniformed officer and another man in a well cut pin-striped suit crowded into it.

The Chief Superintendent indicated a chair; the only space left in Brough's cramped empire.

"Sit down, Harry. Mr Chalfont is here to talk about our dead Civil Servant."

Angel's cab was parked along the southern boundary of Hyde Park. A mounted police officer trotted past without giving it a glance.

Freimann was reading the papers from Morden's briefcase. The other man looked nervous as though awaiting a blood test.

Freimann was scanning the papers. He read English as he spoke it, quickly and efficiently, if a little coldly.

"We need to be sure this is genuine."

"It's real," Morden pursed his lips, "we have proof."

Freimann kept reading. He looked up.

"How did you come by this?"

Morden looked edgy and some of his earlier confidence faded, but Freimann was not finished.

"I have met the author, Howard Crosse, many times. He is a patriotic man. Where did this come from?" Even in strange surroundings, Freimann's voice carried his authority.

Morden studied the German, as Freimann stared back, and made a decision.

"That's our business. We got a deal?"

The German looked at Morden, who smiled back as though any answer would be wrong. For the first time, Freimann felt the stirrings of unease. The small Londoner examined his well-manicured fingernails.

Brough rubbed his hands together to ward off the unwelcoming chill of the morgue. Brough studied Vicki's face as she stared down at Preston's profile. Her face registered nothing; no flicker, no emotion, no colour. Any more than Preston's did.

"Miss Farrow. Vicki? Why did he have Tony Pinner's cab?"

No response from Vicki.

"I need your help, Vicki. I need to find them."

Vicki looked back at Preston. She touched his face; a gesture of gentleness.

"Them."

Pinner was driving, approaching the northern boundary of the Square Mile. At a junction, his eyes quickly scanned the number plate of a taxi across the street. Then he checked out another one.

For Pinner, black cabs had become a thing of menace.

Usher's the Bookmakers had the welcome of a funeral parlour; small groups of men grieving over the last race. It was crying out for someone to pay tribute to the horse that lost.

The nags were racing, their progress recounted from a small Wireless perched on the counter. A group of men clustered near it to hear the whispered placings. The volume was so low that the men were angled respectfully to hear the bad news as it happened.

Tucked away from the losers, Kensal was studying a crossword at a table by the window. Betting slips were scattered around him like dead chess pieces, when a shadow fell across his paper.

"Any joy?"

Kensal looked up.

"Six across. AWOL."

Pinner smiled and sat down, but he was serious again in a breath.

"You heard about Preston?"

Kensal shrugged and shook his head sadly. "Daft Jock. Police were here looking for you. It was your cab he was driving. No insurance and well over the limit."

"Drunk?"

"Dead, in your bloody ticker."

Kensal pointed his finger at Pinner.

"I need your help, Toby."

Kensal shifted in his seat.

"I figured that. What you into, Tone?"

"It's about Crosse, the bloke that I saw, my regular. He was some kind of boffin. Had a brief case with him. He'd just had a meeting or was going to one with the Prime Minister."

Kensal snorted, but Pinner looked at so him sharply that Kensal swallowed his guffaw and waved for Pinner to continue, a stubby pencil still in his newsprint-stained fingers.

"Someone snatched him. I spoke to his Mrs."

Kensal was amazed. "My best mate is Sherlock Holmes."

"I need you to check on my parents, and Anthony."

Kensal looked at his friend with compassion and nodded.

"Where can I reach you? Where's Olympia?"

Pinner rose.

"On this number."

The two men shook hands. Kensal watched Pinner go, before turning back to the crossword.

Brough was sitting uncomfortably in a Whitehall hallway, a cold cavernous corridor, the size of a small country church. A male secretary was working at a desk by a large wooden door. Brough had been there almost seven minutes, when an intercom buzzer went off and the secretary looked up towards the detective.

"You may go in now, Inspector."

Brough nodded and rose to his feet. At the huge door, he was unsure whether to knock or not. The secretary smiled as if he had seen this uncertainty before. Jumped-up tosser. Brough straightened his spine and walked in without knocking. He found himself in a huge, dated drawing room, the office of a Senior Civil Servant, in which Sir Alistair Latimer sat at his desk. Piles of papers covered the desk's surface like wallpaper. Pictures of former incumbents arrayed the walls, all bearing imposing Victorian frowns.

Latimer looked up at Brough's entry. He rose and met the policeman in front of his desk. His movements were smooth, a man who could still play a mean game of tennis. His height and languid air added to his sense of capability. The Guards' tie confirming Brough's assessment.

"Detective Inspector. Thank you for calling in."

"Sir."

Latimer indicted a chair and Brough sat down, feeling the smooth worn leather of its padded arms. He wondered which of the portraits had introduced these chairs. Latimer stayed perched on the corner of his desk, a wide, dark wooden antique. Brough waited. He didn't meet senior Whitehall Mandarins every day, but he knew enough to let them do the talking.

"Do you follow the markets, Inspector? The stock market?"

"On my salary, sir?"

"Touché."

Latimer reappraised Brough. Mind sharper than his attire.

"Howard Crosse worked as a Special Advisor to the Chancellor's Office."

Latimer paused, as if deciding on his direction.

"Although, he advised the Chancellor's Office, Crosse was the PM's man."

Brough studied the answer.

"Can you be more specific? What was he working on?"

"Crosse served as an analyst. He observed trends and looked for icebergs. I think that's the best way to put it."

Brough waited for more while Latimer adjusted his cuffs. Seconds crawled past before Latimer came to a decision.

"London is the financial centre of Europe.

"Primus inter Pares. It is uniquely positioned, a balance, a bridge, a check, between our European brothers and our American Cousins. "

Latimer paused again as if he was unaccustomed to providing these kinds of answers. There was a hint of resentment to his voice. An undercurrent that Brough did not miss.

"Yes, other countries have markets, but London is Number One. That hegemony, London's dominance, is owed in part to the Pound Sterling."

Latimer looked to see that Brough was following his lecture. Brough was.

"However, pressure to jettison the pound has mounted in recent years. Not publicly, of course. Howard Crosse was the Prime Minister's Bishop. The mastermind behind plans to replace it."

Covering his shock, Brough nodded for Latimer to continue.

"As a Civil Servant, I take no view on this. However, when decimalisation is introduced, foreign investors could make billions. Advanced knowledge could cost our economy dear. Some would say, we would have scored an own goal," Latimer hesitated, but he was too far in now.

"Crosse was due to meet with a high-powered delegation of European bankers. The meeting was to have taken place in shadow, Inspector. Then Crosse disappeared."

Latimer waited for Brough this time.

"Now it's all in the news."

Latimer nodded at his pupil.

"His disappearance, his death and the delegation's arrival. Someone does not want the Prime Minister to realise his dream."

Brough nodded slowly, but waited for the punch line. There was one coming. Even in the dry Mandarin's tone, Brough could sense it.

"What we do not want is for interests outside this country to capitalise on this situation."

Latimer leaned forward. He was now much closer to Brough.

"London must remain Number One, Inspector. It could cost this country billions; not just today or tomorrow, but for decades to come."

Brough frowned as he tried to take in Latimer's meaning.

"Sir?"

"Are you making much progress, Detective Inspector? With your enquiries, I mean," Latimer leaned away, pulling himself back from revealing too much, it seemed to Brough.

"Yesterday, a taxi driver was fished out of the Thames."

Brough seemed surprised by his own words.

For the first time, Latimer looked perturbed.

"This has something to do with Crosse?"

Brough shrugged, but it was an affirmative.

"It is possible. They may be connected. May I speak with the Prime Minister?"

Latimer laughed. He seemed genuinely amused.

"I'm afraid not."

Latimer held up a palm.

"I don't see how that would help your enquiries."

Brough rose.

"A man's life may be at stake."

Latimer was undaunted.

"Find whoever killed Howard Crosse, Inspector. Find out what they know and find out how we can stop them."

"Stop them, sir?"

"Thank you for your time, Detective Inspector."

The policeman had been dismissed.

Brough turned away, already reaching into his coat to

pull out a cigarette. As he arrived at the door, Brough lit the cigarette with an air of defiance.

Behind him, Latimer was adjusting his cuff, as he watched him leave.

Pinner had always liked libraries. As a child, he had come to Bethnal Green Library with his granddad. They'd choose one book and then read it together. Pinner tried to remember when that ritual had died out.

Olympia moved across to a table carrying a block of The Financial Times, bound together in a heavy leather tomb. Pinner was sitting reading through material. He looked up exasperated.

"Don't even know what I'm looking for."

Olympia shook her head; a gesture of stubbornness. It came to Pinner, that although scared, Olympia was drawing on this. She was determined – up for it. It was a glimmer of the plucky young singer who had barged her way into an audition, their band and, later, his bed.

"Keep looking," she told him.

Morden and Angel were walking across St James's Park. It was not a relaxing stroll, as Angel stopped, tense.

"Why can't it be cash?" Anxiety strained his voice, altering its pitch.

Morden paused, taking in the park, the riding tracks,

the Park Warden's van, his eyes finally resting on the other man.

"That's not the way they work."

Angel and Morden shared the same look. Uncertainty. It's a killer.

The Melon Café was a well-known haunt of cabbies south of the river. Originally named the Prince of Wales, as it had been for many years a public house; before that a brothel.

Following the Abdication Crisis, the landlord, a modern patriot had taken the bold step of renaming it The Nelson. The sign outside still announced it thus, but to the cabbies, whose idea of patriotism was more conservative, it became known as The Melon, out of respect to the publican who had tried to rewrite history.

The talk was a low hum, punctuated by bursts of steam into a tin milk jug and the clink of plates.

The door opened and Morden eased inside. Eyes took him in. Eyes looked away, but that failed to satisfy him.

He stood for a moment then walked over to the counter. The café owner, Russell Wapping, wiped his hands, opened the till and extracted a few crumpled notes. Morden and Russell shook hands. As they did so, Morden leaned in.

"Tony Pinner."

Russell looked back blankly. The pair were standing still holding hands. Morden patted Russell's hand affectionately and Russell nodded. The message had been delivered.

Empty paper cups had formed a ring around Inspector Brough's desk. His small window was open with a makeshift ashtray on the high windowsill; a small misdemeanour rather than a felony.

Brough was going through his notes, spread out among the cups: a picture of Crosse, another of Pinner's waterlogged cab.

A list of words on a page: Crosse, Pinner, Taxis, Treasury, Chancellor and the Collector.

Brough tapped some ash off his fag. His eyes followed the trail of smoke.

"What did you see, Tony?"

Olympia shivered again as she emptied soup packets into two mugs and added boiling water from a rattling old kettle.

Pinner was sitting on a very old settee. She walked across and passed him a steaming mug. A small gas fire threw out bright light, but scant heat.

"Could it be any colder?"

Pinner smiled.

"It's not safe, anywhere. They found Preston."

Olympia stared at Pinner.

"Who are they, Tony? Do you think they…"

She couldn't finish the sentence. Olympia began to cry. "God. I gave him the keys."

Slowly, her crying subsided.

"I need to speak to my dad."

Olympia looked perplexed at that.

"My dad. He knows. Him and Moshie, they're all I've got."

Olympia looked at him.

"Got me."

Pinner looked up. He stared at Olympia as though he hadn't seen her for a long time. He took her hand. She studied his touch. Pinner drew her to him, but Olympia halted him.

"Stop."

Pinner froze.

"Soup's hot."

Olympia smiled and, putting both her soup and Pinner's aside, before she leaned in and kissed him.

Angel's cab pulled up across the road from Olympia's, but the café was closed. Angel got out, walked up and tested the door. It was firmly locked.

He kicked the door in frustration. Looking back at the café, it occurred to Angel that it had simply been abandoned. He wouldn't have been surprised if it had started to sink.

Pinner's cab drew up opposite Goodge Street Tube Station. Olympia climbed out and turned to talk through the open front driver's window.

"Got it all?" he asked.

Olympia nodded, but she had something to say, too.

"Be careful. I mean it."

However, Pinner shooed her on her way. He watched as she entered the underground station. Olympia turned and waved briefly. Pinner smiled back.

He looked up and down the street, his eyes alighting on black cabs, quickly scanning their number plates. Reassured slightly, he drove off.

A black cab was leaving the hospital entrance. From the gloom of a bus nearby stop, Olympia watched it go.

Olympia walked into the main entrance. She studied the ward map on the wall and joined the queue for the elevator.

The elevator opened and out stepped Olympia and a hospital orderly looking as tired as her uniform. Olympia made her way along the corridor. As she approached the ward, she spied Beth, talking to a man who could only be the police officer Pinner had told her about. The Bow Tie Bobbie. A nurse was hovering nearby.

Olympia checked, then moved down another ward. When she edged back out, they had moved further down the corridor, their backs to her.

Olympia slipped through the curtains surrounding Harold's bed. It was in darkness. Olympia hesitated, then reached out and flicked the small side lamp on.

Harold stared straight at her. Olympia had trouble breathing. So had Harold … he was dead.

In Usher's, Harry the bookmaker answered the phone. Only Harry was permitted to lift the receiver in his establishment.

It was answered in grunts. Kensal was sitting by the window, studying the form and the weather. He was called over to the phone.

"Kensal, it's your mucker." Harry made it sound like a long grunt.

Kensal looked put out and conscious that people were looking at him. He accepted the phone and listened to the urgent voice.

"Yeah? Yeah. No worries. Fine. See you there."

Pinner's cab eased up at Euston Station. Pinner looked up and down the street. He drove slowly past the entrance, turning away from the taxi rank up ahead and into a quiet side street – a deserted narrow alleyway.

Pinner climbed out and approached the railway station via a small side entrance, where rows of postal trolleys had been abandoned: flotsam and jetsam of the industrial dispute.

Pinner walked slowly, almost idling, but alert.

He stopped on the edge of the concourse. Standing beneath the departures board was Toby Kensal, newspaper in hand, bedecked in a bold brown three-piece pinstripe.

Pinner smiled with relief and started walking towards him. The concourse was crowded. Pinner had to step around passengers, whose heads were angled towards the departures board.

Kensal raised his hand in greeting. Pinner quickened his step. Kensal waved again as Pinner reached within five yards of him.

Pinner and Kensal shook hands, as Pinner followed Kensal's gaze. On one side of the station, Morden was moving through the crowd. Pinner looked across to see Angel making his way along the other side of the concourse.

Pinner squared his shoulders and looked at Kensal.

"Sorry, Toby. We're in trouble."

"No mate. You are."

Pinner stared at his friend. Kensal inclined his head slightly; a sad admission.

"On the blue, four and eight, 48."

Pinner did not move as the truth punched him in the sternum.

"You're The Collector."

"Goes with the suit." Kensal indicated the pinstripes.

Pinner glanced back as Morden and Angel closed in. Pinner looked past Kensal, then exploded out of the blocks, knocking Kensal aside.

With a shout, Morden and Angel gave chase, but the station was crowded and crisscrossing streams of passengers blocked and hindered them. Pinner looked to be heading back to the exit that he had come in from as Morden and Angel raced to head him off, barging into people, knocking them over, to a chorus of curses and shouts.

Suddenly, Pinner changed direction. Gathering speed he hurdled the ticket barrier, past a stunned guard.

"Hey!"

Morden and Angel followed. Angel, the bigger man, less successfully, but Morden was faster and clear. As Angel struggled, the guard reached him, taking hold of his jacket.

Angel hit the guard low and the man crumpled, but hung on to Angel's trouser leg.

Pinner charged down towards the platform with Morden in pursuit. A train was waiting to depart. Pinner checked, then cut back and stopped behind a wagon train of mail pallets and trolleys.

Pinner took a steadying breath; a deeper one. Then, Pinner was back in the boxing club waiting for the bell. He could smell the leather of the gloves, the Vaseline smeared on his cheeks and forehead and years of sweat that had formed on the walls and ceilings. Gyms aged like pubs, but it was graft not smoke that did it.

Pinner dropped down. He peered from knee level, as Morden's legs appeared. His shiny shoes were a giveaway. Morden looked confused, looking down the track, across the other platforms. He turned and spied the small mail wagons on the platform. He edged closer.

"Come on, Tony. Be a sport."

Pinner watched from the shadows. Sweat had formed on his face. He watched the feet. Morden was now level with the second wagon.

The mail sack struck him in the face and he keeled backwards.

A metal object hit the floor.

Pinner stooped and picked it up. It was a reflex action. He turned the gun in his hand. He looked shocked, then turned his attention to Morden as his pursuer struggled to his knees. Pinner hit him in the stomach, then landed a tight hook, and Morden went down, the air slammed out of him.

Pinner, working his way back, watched the exit, and moved quickly.

Pinner made his way through the station, adjusting his course towards the exit; British Transport Police to his right, but no sign of Angel.

Pinner exhaled as he hit the sunlight and turned into the shadowed side street.

Angel formed a one-man waiting committee. He was leaning on his cab, scanning the street, as Pinner came out of the station. Angel's cab was parked close to Pinner's, almost kissing it. Angel looked for Morden to be following, but there was only Pinner.

Angel straightened, readying. He was conscious of people walking past on the street. Pinner waved him away from the cab, but Angel stood still. He shook his head and smiled.

Pinner's arm came up, holding Morden's gun. Angel's eyes narrowed as Pinner trotted towards him.

"Keys!"

Angel shook his head again. It was a form of denial. Pinner

stopped and stared at him. A couple stumbled past and froze fixing on the pair, who faced each other like gunfighters.

"Keys!"

Angel moved his hand into his jacket. Pinner swallowed. His finger closed on the trigger. The window of Angel's cab exploded.

A man walking past screamed. Angel covered his head. Pinner waved the gun again. Angel threw him a set of keys. Onlookers froze in fear. One had the presence of mind to throw herself to the ground.

"Both of 'em."

Angel threw the other set of keys. Pinner knelt to scoop them up. Keeping the gun on Angel, Pinner reached his cab and climbed in.

As Pinner drove off, the gun still pointing at Angel, the other man wiped a thin line of blood from his cheek, sliced open where glass from the shattered window had caught him. He turned as Morden staggered out of the dark passageway and lurched towards him. Morden's face was stretched white with rage. He pushed past a cowering couple, striking one of them.

Pinner's cab pulled up in a narrow side street, but he kept the engine idling. Pinner leaned back and steadied his breathing. He looked across at the gun resting on the gearbox. Pinner reached across and lifted the gun into the glove compartment.

"Christ."

Brough was sitting next to Beth in the stark hospital corridor. She had her arms crossed around herself, hugging her chest.

"He's our only lead. Mrs Pinner?"

Beth stared straight ahead.

Brough started to light up, but a dark look from a passing nurse stopped him. Beth smiled at the policeman's embarrassment.

"My Harold, he always had a smoke when he was thinking. I never knew the boy. The dead one."

"Twenty-four. From Scotland. He was learning to be a cabbie."

"Long way from home."

Beth considered this.

"I don't know where he is. He came to see you. You could have helped."

Brough acknowledged the point.

"Now the boy's dead. Harold's dead."

"Nothing's to say. . ."

Beth looked at him for the first time.

"Don't kid yourself. Excuse me."

Brough watched as Beth navigated her way to the toilet, waiting to hold the door open for a young woman.

Beth leaned against the wash hand basin waiting for a cubicle to become free. She nodded to another young woman, busy washing her hands.

"Britain's favourite pastime."

The girl smiled, unsure if the old women meant queuing or hand washing. Old women were like that.

A cubicle emptied and Beth gave the girl a last smile.

Beth locked the cubicle door, put the seat lid down and sat on it.

The world stood still for her; the sound of the other cubicle toilet flushing, the lock being undone and the door opening. Strangely, these mundane sounds were a comfort to her. Beth listened to the tap going on and off, then the door closing. Beth waited, but there were no more sounds.

"Beth?"

Beth sat bolt upright with shock at the woman's muffled voice.

"What? Who is it?" A tremor to her voice; the sound of steps moving nearer the cubicle door.

"Me. Olympia."

Beth looked down at her hands. They were shaking so much that she struggled to open the bolt. Olympia stared in at her. The two women grasped each other's hands, then held each other close.

Brough looked up as Beth returned to her seat. She looked as if she has been crying.

Brough stood gallantly.

"Can I offer you a lift home?"

"I'll get a cab," came the curt reply.

Beth's house was in darkness. The phone rang. It kept ringing, echoing through the deserted house.

Beth sat almost unnaturally upright in the back of Pinner's cab. She looked at her son's eyes in the driver's mirror.

"He's dead, son. Your dad's gone."

Pinner's hands gripped the steering wheel. Beth's hand clasped Pinner's shoulder.

"He didn't have a bad bone in his body," she added.

Pinner's face was set.

"You'll be next, son."

Pinner, on autopilot, flicked the indicator and brought the cab to a halt. Sitting in the shadowed rear seat, Beth was trying not to sob.

"I have to drop you here, mum."

Beth nodded into her hands.

"I'll be round for a cuppa when I've sorted this out."

Beth clambered out of the cab.

"Mum, take the bus next time, eh?" Pinner made his tone light, but he meant the caution.

Beth smiled, but got the message. She leaned in to the window.

"You fix 'em, son. Fix 'em."

Beth, still in her coat, walked through the dark house, a little lost in its stillness. She was standing in front of Harold's chair when the phone rang, making Beth jump slightly. Slowly, with a sense of dread, she picked up the receiver.

"Yes."

Morden's voice was a muffed whisper, as though he was standing behind her.

"How's your grandson, Mrs Pinner?"

CHAPTER 11

THEY HAD VENTURED OUT TO STOCK UP ON supplies.

After what had happened to Preston, they had agreed to stick together. Plus, Pinner felt he owed it to Vicki and Olympia had insisted.

The new supermarket had been chosen because of its high profile. Perhaps it was overkill, but it reassured Pinner. The image of Vicki's drained face as she had been led away by the Police and the wrecked skeleton of his beloved FX3 haunted him.

Pinner was acting as sentinel, parked in the car park, his engine turning over gently.

Olympia and Vicki, together with Anthony, were carrying bags towards Olympia's red Mini. As they reached it, a cab drew up. Pinner was at the window.

"Olympia!"

Olympia stared in confusion at him as she started to move towards Pinner's cab.

Along the row of cars behind her, Pinner could see the burnt orange TAXI sign of a black cab, approaching like a shark fin. Vicki was looking around anxiously. The bags dropped from her hands as she pointed at another cab that had entered the car park. Its SE1 2JY plate marked it out.

Then Pinner spotted the second cab.

"Get out of here!"

Olympia froze, locked between hearing Pinner, but not taking in his meaning. However, Vicki was thinking clearly. A cold calmness had settled over her since Preston's death, giving her a numb clarity. Vicki grabbed Olympia's arm and turned to Pinner.

"Get out of here. Go! I'll see to her."

He watched as Vicki dragged Olympia and Anthony into Olympia's car.

Pinner gunned the engine as a cab came into view and swung the wheel.

Olympia watched in her side mirror as Pinner's cab swerved past a car and turned sharply. She was still watching as another cab accelerated after Pinner's taxi. Anthony was kneeling at the back window.

She turned to Vicki.

"What?"

"Come on, get moving. Now!"

Olympia hesitated. This was all wrong, not real. Anthony turned to look at Vicki. Olympia noticed that a cab has pulled up behind her and felt her chest tighten as Angel stepped out of it.

"Shit!"

Olympia's gunned her engine and as Angel approached the mini leapt into the empty space in front of her. Shocked, Angel turned and ran back to his cab.

Pinner's cab shot out of a junction. Morden's cab followed as the lights changed. The toot of angry horns followed them.

Olympia, looking worried, drove slowly as she reached the exit to the car park.

Vicki pointed ahead.

"Straight across!"

Olympia hesitated for a second, but did as she was told. She looked back in the mirror. Angel's cab was back in view.

Pinner checked his mirror, as he turned the cab sharply into a side street and accelerated.

"Let's see how much you know."

In the chasing cab, Morden was driving. He looked agitated and out of place behind the wheel. He swung the wheel, following Pinner.

Vicki looked around. Behind her, Anthony was sitting in the middle of the back seat watching her. That seemed to calm her.

"At the next junction, turn right into Hackney Road Street, then on past Queensbridge Road, then we'll take Cremer Street."

Olympia looked at her in disbelief.

"What…"

"Keep going. Right now."

Anthony clapped his hands in excitement.

"Right, mum!"

Olympia swung the wheel.

"Now, straight across Kingsland, then…"

"Why don't you bloody drive?" demanded Olympia.

"Never passed my test. This one. Now first right, into Hoxton and across the junction."

As Angel swung his cab around the corner, The Caller crackled on the radio.

"Caller to SE1 4PN, Angel, what's your status?"

Angel picked up the receiver.

"Crossing Hoxton. I've got them in sight."

"Morden?"

The radio voice switched; Morden's thin, almost whispered tones.

"Approaching Whitechapel, he's cutting down towards Mile End."

"Stay with them both."

Silence. The Caller had gone.

Just as Olympia's car approached a wide junction, the lights began to change.

Vicki kept pointing. This was their chance.

"Don't stop."

"The lights…"

"Straight across."

Olympia hit the gas and Anthony shouted with glee.

Olympia's car shot across the junction, swerving

to miss other traffic, Olympia wrestling with the small steering wheel.

Angel watched the lights start to change and smiled. It disappeared as Olympia's car leapt forward going over the red light.

"Shit."

Angel frantically changed gear and accelerated, wildly overtaking a car between them.

Angel's cab powered across the junction.

Angel saw a car and another cab coming towards him. In panic, he spun the wheel.

Angel's cab shot across the road, connecting with the side of another car.

Angel recovered and swung the wheel the other way.

"Right!" He would get them now.

Angel slammed on the brakes, sending his chest thudding into the steering wheel. He looked up, dazed, but with his panic receding.

Standing three feet in front of his cab were a young mother and her child both frozen, staring at him.

He ran his hands over his face.

"Sweet Jesus."

The young mother swept up her child as Angel's cab went into reverse.

Olympia was staring straight ahead, while Vicki was looking backwards and forwards. Anthony was up on his seat.

"What's happening?" breathed Olympia.

"He's gone mum, we lost him."

The women exchanged a look of disbelief and relief.

"Second right and left down City Road at the roundabout."

Olympia looked across at Vicki.

"Vicki, that…"

Vicki's hands gripped the dashboard.

"Christ. I'm gonna puke."

Pinner's cab was being closely followed by Morden's taxi and the distance between them was rapidly shortening.

Pinner looked in his mirror then at the speedometer – 45mph. His car passed a 30mph sign and he eased his foot off the pedal.

"Think, Tony." Speed was not the key here; knowledge was.

A hundred yards behind Pinner, Morden's face was strained in concentration.

"SE1 2DQ, where are you, Morden?"

Morden picked up the radio.

"Looks like he's heading east."

"Don't lose him."

Morden flicked the radio off. He didn't need to be told that. Tension twisted his face.

Pinner rubbed his forehead, trying to come up with an escape plan.

"A needle in a haystack."

Pinner quickly changed gear and cut across a line of traffic.

Morden's cab followed as Pinner weaved his cab across the traffic flow. Once through a neat gap, Pinner's cab accelerated.

The manoeuvre had gained Pinner slightly more distance on Morden. Then Morden got stuck behind a slowing Routemaster bus. He hit his horn in frustration, then cut out. As he pulled out to overtake the bus, another cab was coming the other way.

Morden saw the cab coming, but did not flinch. Instead he accelerated, pressing down the gas pedal and his horn at the same time.

Panic masked the other driver's face as he desperately turned the wheel to avoid a collision, sending his cab over the kerb and jolting onto the pavement, before hitting a low garden fence.

Morden's cab drove on.

In the distance, Morden could see Pinner's cab turning ahead. He increased his speed to make the same turn as Pinner.

He turned the wheel, cutting across the traffic and stopped. In front of Morden was a sea of black cabs.

He faced a huge parking area and garage that dealt

solely in black cabs, with taxis entering and leaving from several different exits.

Looking pale and dazed, Vicki was sitting on the lock up's old couch. She looked shaken. Olympia was with her, her arm around the younger woman, while Anthony was exploring the lock up. They all tensed at the sound of a car pulling up and turned to the door as it opened framing Pinner in the doorway. Anthony ran to him.

Pinner swept his son into his arms. Olympia and Vicki watched them; very different expressions on their faces.

"You have to get out of London. Tonight. All of you," said Pinner as he put Anthony down.

At that, Olympia's frustration and bewilderment boiled over.

"Leave London. Just like that. Anthony's got choir practice tomorrow," Olympia checked as reality hit her low. "OK. I know."

"You're not safe. Not with me."

She looked at Pinner with alarm.

"Tony!"

"Because of something I saw."

Pinner looked across at Vicki.

"I'm fine."

Olympia edged closer to Pinner.

"What did you see?"

Pinner shook his head.

"I don't know. Not yet. But you and Ant are leaving

London. I can't deal with this if I'm worrying about you both. And Vicki."

Olympia shook her head and stepped closer to Pinner.

"No. No more hero stuff. Vicki can take Anthony. There's your mum to think about, too."

That shook Pinner. Olympia took hold of his arm to make her point, binding herself to him with the gesture.

"They go. We stay."

CHAPTER 12

Inside Spitalfields Market, barrows, piled high with fruit and vegetables, were being pulled by bow-legged porters. Cold air for breath at 5am.

Spitalfields was the heart of London's East End. Named after St Mary's Spital, a medieval priory and hospital, it was now a huge all-night wholesale food emporium.

Stacks of produce were piled up; towers of colours and shapes from all over the world. Angel and Morden walked down the aisles. They approached a stall.

They were expected. The Collector, Toby Kensal, now in a grocer's overall, turned to study them.

"He's not pleased. Says Pinner's a resourceful young man. But, you…"

The Collector stabbed a finger at Angel.

"You lost the kid. That, he says, was carelessness and carelessness costs lives. Follow me."

As they walked, Angel mouthed, 'carelessness costs lives' to Morden, who shook his head in caution and looked up at the window ahead at the east side of the market. A figure was watching them from there.

Kensal stopped to admire a melon. With his fist he smashed it. Morden and Angel froze. Kensal looked at the pulp oozing from his fingers.

"Who did for Harold Pinner? It was the Caller's shout."

He turned to face Morden and Angel.

"Ambition is the eighth deadly sin, he says."

Kensal studied the other two men. "This was to stay within the Order. Pretty soon the whole world will know."

Kensal wiped the mess off his hands. He signalled and Alan, the man who had almost come to blows with Pinner in The Crown a few days earlier, opened a small steel door. Kensal indicated for Morden and Angel to enter. They hesitated, but only for a second, then complied.

To their surprise, they stepped into a chiller. Hanging from the ceiling was Mr Freimann; white-faced with cold and terror. He wriggled frantically when he saw Morden and Angel.

"I see you've met."

Alan closed the door behind them as Morden and Angel re-assessed their situation.

Kensal tapped Mr Freimann's chest. It scared the shit out of him.

"Bankers have changed. No more Mr Mainwaring. Now, it's all about information. Knowledge."

Kensal's smile was a sad one, as if confiding about a family loss.

"Mr Freimann has shared his with us. Seems you boys were making plans, some sort of private enterprise, without our knowledge?" He received no answer.

"A spot of freelancing, eh, boys?"

Kensal started to pull on his leather gloves. That focussed the two younger men. Morden and Angel did not take their eyes off him.

"Yours was a simple task. Warn off Pinner. Make sure he forgets. No more mistakes. He's called time. You have 24 hours."

Kensal smoothed his gloves over his meaty knuckles.

"You have been heavy-handed. Now you must clean up your own mess. Everyone who has any knowledge of Crosse must be dealt with. Everyone."

Kensal made his point to Morden, who nodded.

"Everyone," agreed Morden.

Morden and Angel turned to go.

"One more thing. Remember your oath. Say goodbye, Mr Freimann."

Freimann struggled frantically as the two men turned away from him. They knew dead meat when they saw it.

Brough was sitting having another cup of dreadful coffee and toying with his lighter. He picked up another sheet of typed paper. 'The Missing Persons' register. He scanned down the list: Crosse, Howard – Civil Servant. Brough had written 'Treasury' next to the name.

He scanned further down: Freimann, Lothar – Financier; nationality – West German.

Brough turned his lighter over and picked up a phone.

"Arthur, Brough here. What's the story of this missing German?"

"The banker? He arrived from Frankfurt. Climbed into a cab. Not seen since."

Brough tapped his lighter.

"What kind of banker?"

A pause, from Arthur in Records.

"Er… It's here – a currency specialist."

"What kind of cab?"

"Just a black one."

Brough snapped open his lighter and the long flame spurted skyward.

Morden and Angel approached a sparkling new cab parked outside Spitalfields Market in Brushfield Street. A pile of used crates burned nearby, a beacon of warmth to those who spent their evenings exposed to London's black nights.

Angel looked across at the smaller man for guidance.

Morden knew what to do.

"Pinner's mum. Let's try the old girl first, then the copper."

Detective Inspector Brough was at Beth's door. It opened before he could reach it, but Beth had the chain on.

"I can't help you, Inspector."

"Tony can."

"No."

"Tell him, I know why."

"I can't. I don't know where he is."

"Yes, you do."

Pressed against the inner hallway wall, Olympia was listening to the exchange from behind Beth's back and trying not to breath.

Angel and Morden looked across as Brough turned away from the door as it closed on him. They both leaned back in their seats as he climbed into his police car. Morden tapped Angel on the shoulder and they followed Brough's Rover.

Victoria Coach Station failed to live up to the regal nature of its name. It was a stark concrete cave. Pinner was kneeling, hugging his son beside a noisy, grimy coach. Vicki was standing, looking nervous. Over Anthony's shoulder, Pinner spied a police constable. Walking in front of the officer were Olympia and Beth. As they turned towards Pinner, the policeman walked the other way. Pinner exhaled slowly as Beth followed his gaze.

Pinner stood and collected his son and their bag.

"Get on the bus, mum."

"They're after you, too." Beth's eyes were still on the police officer's receding back.

Pinner moved them towards the coach door.

"An evacuee. After all these years." Beth shook her head sadly

Pinner did not answer. He was past nostalgia. He ruffled Anthony's hair and he was rewarded with a bright smile. Anthony launched himself into Olympia's arms.

Looking over her shoulder at Beth. Olympia guided Anthony's hand into his grandmother's. The two women nodded to each other.

Vicki, Beth and Anthony climbed onto the bus.

Pinner was standing with his hands in his coat pocket, Olympia beside him.

Beth looked back at the two of them from the bus steps, as Vicki guided Anthony into a seat. Excited by the prospect of a coach trip, he started waving from the bus.

As the bus departed in a plume of oily fumes, Pinner and Olympia turned away and headed towards his cab. As they walked, she reached for his hand. He nodded slowly. They climbed into the cab, Pinner scanning the street and nearby junction.

"I'll drop you around the corner. Remember what I said."

"What about you?" Olympia asked, plainly worried.

"Time I caught up with an old friend."

Pinner looked in the side mirror. A police constable was approaching. Pinner started the engine and moved off cautiously.

The police officer watched them go, before a gaggle of tourists surrounded him asking the way to Buckingham Palace.

Pinner fed coins into the payphone slot, as he listened to the connection and dialling tone. The telephone box stank of stale cigarettes and urine, but Pinner paid no heed.

A woman's voice answered on the fourth ring.

"Hello?"

Pinner covered his mouth.

"Listen. This is a message for Toby Kensal."

"Who is…""

"Tell him – Pinner's found out the truth about Crosse."

Pinner put down the receiver and walked back to his cab. The door to the red phone box closed slowly on the empty booth.

Pinner's cab was parked up across from the Golden Hart's entrance. He looked at his watch. As a cabbie, he was well-schooled in the art of waiting. The pub door opened and Kensal came hurrying out. He looked slightly unsteady on his feet, but he unlocked his cab and got in.

Kensal's cab moved off and Pinner followed, with Olympia in the back.

Brough was standing in front of Harold Pinner's old lock up. He tried the door: locked. He pulled out a set of skeleton keys out of a deep coat pocket and started to work his way through them. Twenty years in the Met had given him a unique set of skills; breaking and entering was one.

Pinner's cab was stationary outside Smithfield Market. He was watching where Kensal's cab squatted on the roadside.

Brough switched on the light and looked around the damp lock up; an old cab under a heavy canvas dustsheet cover, paint tins, a discarded set of licence plates, dirty mugs still waiting to be washed up. He touched the side of the kettle. Still warm. Someone had been here earlier today. Pinner.

Pinner's cab was in shadow opposite Smithfield's grand Victorian facade. Pinner watched as Kensal, The Collector, climbed into his cab and drove off.

He started to get out of his cab.

"Stay with the car. Front seat."

Olympia climbed out and considered the man before her. She pulled him forward to share a strong kiss.

Olympia broke off and turned leaning into the cab driver's seat.

Pinner looked down. In Olympia's hand was Morden's gun.

Pinner stood at the old door. He pressed the doorbell and waited. After a moment, he could hear the sound of shuffling feet. Then the door was opened. The nozzle of Morden's gun greeted the figure opening the door.

"You'd better come in."

The feet shuffled backwards. Pinner and his gun followed closing the front door behind him.

Pinner edged down the narrow hallway, up a trio of steps and approached the door to the sitting room.

"Take a seat, Tony. A sherry? I prefer Madeira."

"I'm driving, Moshie."

Moshie Kent laughed; a smoker's cackle.

He moved across and placed the drink by a chair.

"Sit. Enjoy. Life's too short. And put the gun away. Morden's?"

Pinner sat down, but followed neither instruction.

"We made a mistake with you. We past your father over, but you're … you're your mother's boy. 'Course, your grandfather was a great servant. The war changed that. Are you a good listener, Tony?"

Kent made himself comfortable.

"People like to talk. Remember the poster 'Careless talk costs lives'? You're too young. People talk and we listen. They can't help themselves, verbal diarrhoea some of them. We have listened for years. Lots of things happen in cabs.

"Affairs. Betrayals. Deals. Murder."

As Moshie told his tale, Pinner soaked it up.

Rutter's rowing boat was tied up at the bank of the river. King James II was being helped out by the boatman.

His aide followed. The King checked and turned to the boatman.

"London began with the Thames. So did we. Common boatmen." Moshie gave a humble shrug.

The King hesitated then pulled off his small ruby ring and handed it to the boatman. Rutter's huge paw closed on the treasure.

"We, taxi drivers, we started with the Thames. Watermen. Ferrying the rich across the black water."

Two men were lighting torches. They looked up and down the lane. One stepped forward and lit a bundle of tinder at one building. The other moved across to light another. They worked their way down the street, setting it alight. The Street sign read 'Pudding Lane'.

On a boat, the two men looked back at their handiwork as the flames from the fire spread through London.

"We heard it all. Saw some too."

Moshie took another sip.

"Sometimes we even smelled the blood."

A horse's bridle. Breath out of its nostrils.

A horse-drawn cab pulled up outside the pub. A gentleman emerged with a painted woman on his arm. The cabbie noted the gent and prostitute.

The girl, bloodied and battered, was dead on the cobbles. Gentleman with a cane retreated past a sign 'Fournier Street', as the cabbie drew up at the other end of the street.

"Sometimes we spilled it."

Pinner watched Moshie Kent. As the old man spoke, the deeper Pinner was descending into his own dark dreams.

A man was being bundled out of a cab, dragged by two others. The driver watched as they stabbed him. The victim slid down the wall. Bloody graffiti trailing down the brickwork. His assailants climbed back into the cab as the engine was gunned.

Now he woke up to find himself in the same nightmares.

A gentleman climbed into the back of a cab. Elegant grey suit with a flower in the button hole. He pulled out a silver cigarette case, engraved with a coat of arms with the motto 'Ich Dien'.

Pinner shivered. *I serve.*

Moshie was gazing out of his window, lost in his tale. He turned his attention back to the present.

"I knew your grandfather well. Another Harold. What was it he used to say? 'One in the eye'. Ha, ha! Full of mirth, Harold."

Pinner leaned forward.

"Crosse?"

Moshie took a sip of his Madeira.

"We're a patriotic order. During the war, both wars, we helped weed out spies, traitors to Britain. Your grandfather – wasn't happy with some of the methods we employed.

"Thought those days were gone. Then some information comes to light."

"What happened to Crosse?"

Moshie studied his drink then turned his attention to Pinner.

"Know what our masters in Whitehall are planning?

To get rid of the pound; decimalisation is just a ruse. A ruddy smokescreen."

Pinner looked unmoved. Only now were the visions and nightmares fading.

"Britain's heritage sold down the Swanny by our own Prime Minister and some poncy civil servant."

"Tell me, Moshie."

"He doesn't matter. Britain matters. Sunday's papers will be full of revelations regarding our dear Prime Minister. He'll resign and with Crosse and his report AWOL, it'll be business as usual. You haven't touched your drink."

"All this for a pound."

"The pound. Our pound! Our heritage!"

Kent's face was alight, his madness clearly illuminated.

Pinner studied Moshie, then his drink.

"And my dad." It was a quiet statement.

Moshie frowned as he poured himself another.

"I didn't countenance that. Young men are always too ambitious. It's the eighth deadly sin."

Moshie turned to Pinner.

"No one cares anymore, Tony."

"I do. About my family. About Crosse."

"Crosse! You fingered Crosse, Tony."

Pinner looked startled and Moshie pressed his advantage.

"You gave us him. You might as well have trussed him up like a turkey, fattened for Christmas!"

Then, Pinner remembered.

"Toby. In the café."

Moshie nodded.

"Careless talk costs lives."

"No! You did the killing."

Pinner shifted the weight of the gun in his hand, causing Kent's eyes to flick to it. Kent offered Pinner open palms.

"Not on my hands."

Moshie turned to Pinner.

"I have high hopes for you, Tony. You found me, that takes brains and nerve."

Pinner rose in his seat. For a second, Moshie looked fearful then the moment passed.

"I'll think about it."

Moshie smiled.

"You do that, son."

Pinner looked down at the old man.

"I'll see myself out."

"Wait."

Pinner stood as Kent drew a small ruby ring off his finger.

"We still serve."

Kent indicated that Pinner should take the ring. Pinner hesitated, then his hand closed around it.

A disgarded memory resurfaced at the touch of the ring; his granddad taking his hand as a small boy, the cold band a contrast to his grandfather's warm large fingers. Moshie's tale held some truth. Pinner shivered. Too close to home.

He turned at the blare of a horn from outside. Then, a second blast.

Pinner tensed as he heard the front door to Moshie's flat open. Pinner looked into Moshie's face, as the door to the sitting room began to open. Pinner swung around bringing his gun up as Morden and Angel stepped into the room.

They froze; small room, four men, one gun.

Morden smiled.

"Tony Pinner. Like a homing pigeon. You can't kill us all, Tony."

The gun was trained on Morden. Pinner stared down the barrel.

"You're the instrument."

Morden shrugged.

"My father's son."

Pinner looked confused and Morden's smile broadened. Moshie nodded to confirm the truth. Pinner took in the two pairs of shiny black shoes; Moshie's and Morden's. Kent smiled with genuine sympathy.

"You were too busy with your music."

"And your black singer." Morden's smile widened.

Pinner tensed. He stepped closer to Morden, the gun barrel nearer Morden's face.

"You cut me up to get Crosse. Did you do my dad?"

Morden looked from Pinner to his father, Kent. Pinner's gun hand didn't waver. Kent peered into Pinner's face.

"He was an old man, Tony. It comes to us all."

Pinner's eyes were still on Morden. Angel shifted slightly. Pinner nodded his head as though willing Angel to make a move, but at a signal from Kent, Angel stopped.

Pinner stared at Morden.

"You're not."

Morden and Kent both looked confused.

"An old man."

Kent realised Pinner's meaning.

"Tony, please. Consider everything. My offer. You have a boy of your own. This will go no further."

Morden looked across at his father, but Kent was determined to save his son.

"You come to us, when you feel the time is right. We'll not darken your door, you and yours again."

Pinner shifted his weight, his finger flexed on the trigger.

Pinner considered all three faces: Kent was earnest, pleading, but Morden looked back at Pinner like a viper, Angel's expression flat and brutal.

Pinner nodded. He saw his predicament. He moved closer to Morden. Slowly, he moved around nearer the door. Angel and Morden moved with him.

Kent's breath was long.

"Bless you."

Pinner was now nearest the door. Morden's eyes remained fixed on his. Angel's eyes were on the gun.

"I'll see myself out."

Pinner left the sitting room and reached the door.

"My love to your beautiful mother."

Pinner checked at Moshie's words and looked down at the polished shoes by the gas meter at the front door.

Kent raised a glass to Pinner as the front door closed behind him, before he turned back to face Morden and Angel.

"You could learn from him. He's got balls."

Morden looked at his father coldly.

"Always looking for a shortcut, son. This time your ambition has proved too costly. No more freelancing. The Order will not tolerate it."

Morden's face betrayed his resentment and hate, but Kent dismissed him and turned to Angel.

"Call Alan."

Angel did not move. He looked at Morden for confirmation. Kent's eyes bore into his son. Morden nodded to Angel, who picked up the phone.

Moshie was touching his bare finger; Pinner still had the ring.

As Pinner hurried to his cab, Olympia began to climb out.

"In the back!" he shouted.

As Morden and Angel were leaving Moshie's flat, Kent's weathered voice reached them with another rebuke.

"Bring me some good news, next time, son."

Morden checked. His face tense, he looked down at the gas meter by the front door.

"Taxi for Moshie."

His black leather gloves were eased on as he looked back towards the living room.

Pinner was sitting in his cab, staring straight ahead. The Thames stretched out in front of him. He slid out of his cab.

The once beautiful cab that Preston had died in was still there, taped off by the police. Pinner touched the cab as though saying farewell.

He focused on something at his feet. Pinner stooped and picked up a small metal object. In his hand was the Che Guevara pin badge that Preston had always worn. The radical Scot.

Pinner walked to the water's edge, studying the dark water. He made a decision. He turned back to the cab, where Olympia was standing leaning on the bonnet.

As Pinner stopped in front of her and handed her the pin badge, she bit her lip.

"See Vicki gets this."

Olympia nodded.

Tony Pinner was going to war.

Brough was sitting waiting in the dank, drafty lock up, his overcoat wrapped around him. He had dozed off. He woke with a start. First he registered where he was, then that he was not alone. Angel looked at him. A light flicked on to his right. Standing under the other light was Morden.

Brough frowned.

"I'm waiting for someone."

Brough started to rise, but Morden inclined his head, indicating that he should stay still.

Brough looked between them.

"Taxi for Brough." Morden's voice was a chilling whisper.

The cough of a silencer ended the conversation. Brough looked in disbelief at the red spot on his chest.

Angel was driving, while Morden was doing his nails in the back seat.

He leaned forward.

"Toby Kensal will know where to find him."

Angel turned back.

"Then?"

"Then Pinner. Then the world," Morden smiled at his own jest, as he examined his cuticles.

Moshie Kent was asleep in his armchair, an empty glass on the coffee table, when the doorbell rang. Moshie did not respond. The bell rang again.

Alan was banging on the door. It was getting dark outside. Alan looked exasperated and moved closer to the door, making a decision.

Alan tried the door. It was unlocked and he moved inside quickly.

Alan walked past the gas meter and peered into the gloom. In the dusk, he could see Moshie slumped in his armchair.

Alan shook his head.

"Let's have some light on the subject."

He flicked the light switch.

The front door and windows exploded outward. A blistering, wrenching shriek as flames engulfed the building and bricks and shards of glass showered onto the road.

It was race night at Catford Dog Track, bookies and punters milling about as lean muscled dogs were led out for the next race.

Kensal was studying the form. He looked undecided, then stepped towards a bookmaker with his painted leather bag. Pinner was standing some distance higher in the stand, watching him. He knew his friend's habits well. Strange to still call him friend.

Pinner took a step forward, then froze, as he spied Morden and Angel moving in on Kensal.

Kensal handed over his money, but just as the bookmaker handed him his betting stub, Morden stepped forward and took it for Kensal.

Kensal looked from Morden to Angel. This was not Spitalfields, this was Catford and, alone, Kensal sensed his vulnerability. The tables had turned. He looked scared as they led him down the dog tunnel. The dogs were yapping. Kensal was shaking his head, pleading with the other two men, as Pinner watched from across the dust track.

Minutes later, Morden and Angel walked towards their cab.

They had left Kensal sitting on the cold concrete floor against a mesh fence. A friendly dog was licking his face through the mesh, but there was no response from Kensal to this affection.

Morden and Angel reached their cab. They climbed in. Its number plate was SE1 6BF.

When Angel switched on the ignition, the radio came on.

"Two people have died in a house fire in Smithfield Market. Police are investigating the blaze, which they believe was caused by a gas leak."

Angel changed gear and gently moved the cab forward.

Morden smiled to himself.

"Everyone."

Morden took off his black gloves slowly and deliberately, with a sense of exaggerated satisfaction.

Angel's cab was travelling along the road. Behind it, three vehicles back, was Pinner's new FX4 cab.

As they reached a junction a mile or so south of the river, Pinner drew up alongside. He looked straight across at Angel, his face tight.

Angel glanced across to his right.

"Christ! It's him."

Pinner jumped the lights, revving his engine. Angel frantically did the same as Morden was thrown about in the back of the cab.

Within seconds, the two cabs were hurtling along the road. This time there was no regard for the speed limit.

The first cab took a corner recklessly, the second tight

on its tyres. They screeched as tyres scorched and gears were crashed.

Pinner's face was tense as he swung the wheel. He was chanting a litany to himself.

"Dunton Road into. Yeah. Grange. See if you like this, boys."

Pinner wrenched the wheel.

Pinner's cab skidded across a junction. People climbing off a bus, leapt back on to it, as Pinner's taxi burned across the tarmac.

Angel was tugging at his wheel.

"He's a mad man!"

Angel hauled the wheel around.

The people on the bus watched in disbelief as a second cab screamed past.

Morden was thrown against the front glass partition. He was pitched to the side as Angel hugged the wheel and the cab rode sideways again. Morden straightened on the back seat. His mouth was bleeding from the impact.

Morden wiped away the smear, speaking through the blood.

"Don't lose him."

Pinner's cab zipped along the road, dodging a cyclist and rounding a bus. With the minimum of care, Angel's cab streaked after it.

Pinner swung the wheel. A pedestrian stepped out on to the road. Pinner slammed the horn.

The woman froze then fell backwards.

Pinner tightened his grip on the wheel.

"Women pedestrians."

He glanced back in his mirror. Angel and Morden were less than 40 yards behind him.

Pinner looked at his watch.

"Two minutes, boys."

Angel changed gear and the cab groaned around another corner.

Morden's face was against the glass divide.

"Where the hell is he going?"

"How the hell should I know, but he can drive."

Pinner's cab seemed to be accelerating away.

Pinner's face was tense, he looked across at Tower Bridge, then back to his watch.

"One minute."

He pressed the accelerator, then swung the wheel violently.

Pinner's cab hurtled onto the bridge as the barriers started to come down. Angel's cab was on his tail.

Angel and Morden were thrown to one side as the cab lurched around the turn.

"We've got him."

Morden's gaze followed Pinner's cab as the barrier came down behind them.

Pinner took a deep breath. In front of him the bridge was already rising. Rather than slow down, Pinner pressed his foot down on the accelerator.

As the bridge parted and rose, the gap grew. Pinner's cab powered up the incline and shot over the gap as the road surface fell away.

Pinner's arms were locked. His face stretched back as if G-force was pulling it.

Pinner's cab landed with a thud and a howl on the other side.

Pinner recoiled at the impact and wrestled to keep the taxi under control.

Pinner's cab swung and skidded, but he straightened her.

Through the front window, Angel and Morden watched incredulously as Pinner's cab rose and fell.

Disbelief was replaced by terror as the bridge came up towards them.

Morden's clenched fist struck the glass pane at Angel's head.

"Yes! You can make it."

Angel was terrified. Fear engulfed him.

"No!"

As the rising gap widened, Angel's cab shot over. The gap was too great. The cab fell, seemingly in slow motion, plunging into the river. The Thames swallowed it.

Moshie Kent's ruby ring was sitting in Pinner's palm. As it rested in his hand, he could hear his grandfather's warming laughter. In some dark troubling way, the ring was a link to Harold; another side of his grandfather, a side he never knew. *King Harold.*

He took a deep, calming breath, as he turned it over as though weighing it, deciding whether to put it on or not; to claim it as his own.

Instead, he stepped forward and threw it high into the Thames.

Olympia stood behind him, watching carefully, her arms tightly wrapped around her body.

EPILOGUE

Pinner, Olympia and Anthony were walking along Southend's sea front. Pinner and Olympia were holding hands, Anthony skipping around them.

As they entered the pier, Olympia pointed to the ice-cream stall, face alight with joy. The place was quiet. Out of season. Pinner liked it this way.

As they ordered their cones, laughing together, a London black cab slowly made its way along the desolate esplanade. It turned into the opening to the pier and entered the pier. It was being driven very slowly. Unnoticed by Pinner and his family, the driver's face was in shadow, his hands on the wheel and a small ruby ring on his pinky finger.

ACKNOWLEDGEMENTS

FIRST OF ALL, MY GRATITUDE TO:
Douglas and Rosemary for all their support, Alison for keeping me right, Danny and his enthusiasm for Taxi Cabs and The Main Man for his interest in this project throughout its evolution.

Thanks to Gabi Prekop and all the Cambridge crew at SOURCES2.de, Carlos Horillo and Patrick Morcas at El Parador, one of London's lost treasures, The Gentle Author at Spitalfieldslife.com, and Stefan Dickers at the Bishopsgate Institute.

To Lynne Forsyth, a gem of an editor, word-whiz Julie Beedie, Richard Findlay and all the Matador Team.

To Graham Waite at London Vintage Transport Association and the staff at the London Transport Museum.

Also, to Ged and Janet for their faith in this book.

Finally, I'd like to pay tribute to all those who have The Knowledge, and patrol the streets of London, serving this colourful city and it's inhabitants.

ABOUT THE AUTHOR

Mark Jackson is a BAFTA Scotland nominated writer and an award-winning short filmmaker.

He is the author of four books. The screenplay of his first book *The Revenge of Colonel Blood* was an official selection at the Burbank International Film Festival.